THE WORLD EXPLODED

Dingo Whaley and his gang planned simple, direct action: move in fast, move in hard. Don't try anything fancy. Don't try to finesse the gold, just dynamite the building, grab the gold, and get out. Make it like an old-fashioned military raid: no prisoners, just maximum destruction.

And that's just what happened. . . . When they hit town and started throwing dynamite around, they caught the Rangers by surprise. It was only a matter of minutes before the town of San Angelo was leveled.

When Matt found his blood brother, he was lying facedown in the dirt, his head a mass of blood. . . .

WILLIAM W. JOHNSTONE

BLOOD BOND

SAN ANGELO SHOWDOWN

ZEBRA BOOKS
KENSINGTON PUBLISHING CORP.

ZEBRA BOOKS are published by

Kensington Publishing Corp.
475 Park Avenue South
New York, NY 10016

First Printing: February, 1994

Printed in the United States of America

One

Dingo Whaley was the first to spot the vehicle in the distance. He had to squint a little in the bright Texas sunshine and still could not be sure if it was a wagon or carriage.

"What is it, boss? Buffalo?"

"Shut up for a minute, Murdock, and let me think."

Pierce watched the scene from several feet away. He knew that Mel Murdock was not the brightest individual in Texas and would probably not listen to Dingo's command. Pierce didn't like Murdock—almost nobody in the gang did—so he sat back to watch the show. Murdock didn't disappoint him.

Murdock spit a stream of tobacco juice and continued, "Hell, I'm so sick of seeing the rump end of those shaggy beasts, I'd sure like to get the tail end of something a sight prettier! When are we going to hit some town—"

Without a second's hesitation, Dingo reached out and hit Murdock with a solid backhanded slap. Dingo didn't even use his full force, but it knocked the other man out of his saddle. He landed on his feet, started to reach for the gun at his side. Pierce scratched the stubble on his face, laughed softly. Murdock glanced at Pierce, then at Dingo, who was apparently ignoring him. Murdock took his hand away from the gun.

Though both men were over six feet tall and had the well-worn look of buffalo hunters, Dingo was the bulkier of the two. He weighed in at over three hundred pounds of bone and muscle. He was said to be the best fighter and one of the fastest shots in the West. Murdock and other members of his gang knew he was also mean as sin. He was a bad man to tangle with.

"I thought I said to be quiet."

"Sure, boss. I didn't mean to—"

"Just shut up."

Pierce laughed as Murdock got back on his horse and rode off. Pierce had no sympathy for the other man.

Dingo continued to watch the dust in the distance. He finally made out details of a single coach followed by a single rider. If it was

6

another sodbuster, a raid would hardly be worth the effort. A more fancy rig could mean a merchant with a hidden cash box or some merchandise that could come in handy. In any case, Murdock did have a point. Dingo and his men had seen too many damned buffalo. The last big hunt had been just a few days before. It was good money—real good money. But the work was hard and tiring. Now it was time for a different kind of sport and maybe some easier money.

Another member of the gang rode up and stopped beside Pierce. He looked almost frail compared to the larger men, though he was not a small man and closer inspection revealed that he also had been hardened by years of living in the open country.

"What's cooking?" the third man asked quietly.

"Boss is in a cranky mood, Jessup. Wouldn't rile him, if I were you. Murdock made that mistake."

"Again?" He laughed. "You think he'd learn sooner or later."

"I know I don't plan on pissing off Dingo. I value my hide too much."

"Me too. Crossing Dingo Whaley is one thing nobody in their right mind would ever do."

Dingo turned his horse and rode the few feet back to the other two men.

"Jessup, you're familiar with this country. How close would you say we are to the nearest town?"

"There's a settlement or two within a half-day's ride of here." Jessup absently scratched himself as he thought. "The nearest town of any size is San Angelo. Only thing much there is Fort Concho, which means you can buy beer and women."

"I'm more concerned about the law."

"Hell, there may be a Ranger or two. Can't get away from those bastards these days. But the soldiers? The damned fort ain't big enough to have very many, and I'll wager most of those are new recruits who couldn't find their way home with a map. Rangers and soldiers are pretty busy with the Indians and Mexicans, anyway."

"Sounds good to me. Pierce, get the rest of the boys together. We're going to pay us a visit to those pilgrims down yonder."

Sam Two-Wolves shook his head slightly as his horse made its way through rotting corpses at the site of a recent buffalo hunt. The horse was skittish, and the smell was terrible, but Sam's firm hand kept the horse steady.

From several hundred feet away, Matt Bodine sat on his own horse. For once, he made no wisecracks, for he knew the ache that such a sight produced in Sam. He had a similar feeling in his own heart since they shared a common cultural heritage, as blood brothers. For many Indians, the buffalo was the source of life itself, and with the killing of the buffalo their life was also disappearing.

Sam was the son of a great and highly respected chief of the Cheyenne, his mother a beautiful and highly educated white woman from the East who had fallen in love with the handsome chief and married him in a Christian ceremony. As an Indian, Sam was deeply aware of the bond between men and nature, between Indian and buffalo.

Matt was the son of a rancher and met Sam when they were both just kids. The two quickly became friends, with Matt spending as much time in the Cheyenne camp as he was on the ranch at home. They grew up together, and Matt was adopted into the tribe as a True Human Being, according to Cheyenne belief. Matt and Sam were joined by a ritual of knife and fire. Though Matt's background was different than Sam's, he understood his blood brother's feelings better than most.

Their relationship was an easy one, often filled with good-natured kidding, but they could prove to be a terrible foe. On such occasions, Sam's obsidian eyes grew cold and Matt's temper could take hold. Both were young, in their mid-twenties, handsome and muscular, over six feet tall and weighing over two hundred pounds, though Sam's hair was black and Matt's was brown. They worked together individually and as a team, after having survived dozens of fights and shoot-outs in their travels across the west in which they were now earning the reputation of gunfighters.

They came by their fighting ability honestly. Sam's father, Medicine Horse, had been killed during the Battle of the Little Big Horn after he charged Custer, alone, unarmed except for a coup stick. Realizing the inevitability of war, the chief had ordered Sam from the Indian encampment before the battle, to adopt the white man's ways and to forever forget his Cheyenne blood. That was a promise that Sam had a difficult time keeping.

Matt and Sam had witnessed the subsequent slaughter at the Little Big Horn, though that was a secret only they shared. During the time following the death of Sam's father, Sam and Matt decided to drift for a time in an effort to erase the terrible memory of the battle. Though they were often mistaken for out-of-work drifters, in truth the two men were well-educated and wealthy. Sam

Two-Wolves was college-educated, while Matt had been educated at home by his mother, a trained schoolteacher. Sam's mother had come from a rich eastern family and left him with many resources. Matt had earned his fortune through hard work and smart business moves. He rode shotgun for gold shipments and as an army scout, then invested his money in land. Matt and Sam now owned profitable cattle and horse ranches along the Wyoming-Montana border.

"You can't do anything about this now," Matt called out to Sam. "Let's move on."

"I know," Sam answered. "But this is such a waste. I'd like to get my hands on the men that did this."

"Yeah. So would I. But it's all legal, sanctioned and encouraged by the government."

Sam urged his horse down the road at a faster pace. He said, "Let's get out of here before I get sick."

Matt looked around, shook his head, then hurried to catch up. He would give Sam a few miles to regain his natural good humor. Sometimes it was better not to push, and this was one of those times.

Peter Easton shuffled some papers around on the makeshift desk in front of him. His ample stomach made the maneuver difficult. Carl Holz, Easton's assistant, knowing Easton's sensitivity to his weight, said nothing. The carriage shifted on the rocky ground, tossing the papers into the air. Easton tried to grab them, as did Holz.

"Damned! How's a man supposed to get any work done in these conditions!"

"I suggest again, sir, that you might be better off postponing work until you reach Fort Concho," Holz said. "All the pertinent information is in the summary I prepared for you."

Holz was much slimmer than Easton, though his hair was also slicked back and both wore expensive suits. Holz picked up a slip of paper from beneath another stack and handed it to his superior. Easton repositioned his glasses and again read through the report.

"Damned these Mexicans anyway," he said. "They can't control their own bandits and they get upset because one or two of our men cross the border in pursuit. Harumph!"

"One man in particular," Holz corrected. "A Texas Ranger named Josiah Finch." He reached into the stack and pulled out another slip of paper, glanced down a list. "I might point out that the complaints aren't limited to just Mexican authorities. The Department has received complaints from Indian Territory, New Mexico . . ."

"I get the idea. This Ranger doesn't understand limits—though I understand that *all* these Texans think they're too good to follow the rules. I'll conduct my investigation, make my recommendations, and get back to Washington as soon as possible." He looked out the window at the dry countryside. "I'd just as soon be back there now. Damn, I wished I had left that senator's wife alone . . ."

A gunshot that sounded like a cannon suddenly filled the air and a hole exploded in the side of the wagon, filling the inside with splintered wood. This time the papers scattered and nobody bothered to pick them up as the horses spooked and started to run down the road. Easton and Holz hit the floor as another shot made a second hole in the side.

Outside, Dingo Whaley and his men were quickly overtaking the vehicle. The escort on horseback squeezed off a shot at the attackers, who returned the fire. A half-dozen bullets hit him at the same time and he fell to the ground. The driver, not willing to be a hero and be shot for his efforts like the escort had been, tried unsuccessfully to stop the team. Dingo solved that problem by aiming his big buffalo gun at the lead horse and squeezing off a shot. It dropped in its tracks, causing the remaining frightened horses to stumble and fall. The driver flew through the air like a rag doll. Dingo started to take aim, tracking the body as he might a flying duck, then lowered the gun and turned his attention back to the wagon.

The hitch broke and the wagon overturned in a cloud of dust and noise.

It had been many miles since Matt and Sam had left the buffalo carcasses, but Sam was still quiet.

"I could sure go for a hot meal and a cold beer," Matt said. "I'm sick and tired of this trail grub. Why, that breakfast we had this morning was—"

"You cooked breakfast," Sam answered.

"Oh. Right. Well, what about that dinner yesterday . . ."

"You cooked dinner yesterday," Sam answered.

"Damn right! Maybe it's time you did some of the cooking!"

"What? And listen to your griping?"

But Sam smiled, and Matt grinned in return.

"That's more like it," Matt said. "You're mighty poor company when you're in one of your moods."

"*My* moods! Hell, even at my worst, I'm better than you are when you get all goggle-eyed over some saloon singer . . ."

Matt shook his head. "Well, now I've done it! You're back to normal. Me and my big mouth! All you need now is a good fight to put you in a *really* fine mood!"

The shot of a buffalo gun roared in the distance.

"As you were saying, brother, my mood's rapidly improving!" Sam said, as he turned his horse and raced toward the sound.

Matt rolled his eyes toward the sky. "Me and my big mouth!"

Two

Carl Holz touched his forehead and felt wet. He pulled back his hand and saw blood. When he volunteered to assist Easton in his department investigation, as a "favor" to an influential senator, Holz had hoped to make some points for himself to further his career. He had not planned on getting shot at. What had happened? He blinked, and found himself looking into the barrel of a Colt revolver held by one of the biggest men he had ever seen. Others had their guns pointed at Easton.

"Come on out, nice and easy," one of the men said. "I haven't decided whether or not to shoot you. If you cooperate, we might let you walk away."

Holz groaned and pulled himself out of the carriage. Easton was trying to take control, though west Texas and a gang of outlaws were much different than the Washington, D.C., society that he was familiar with. At least a dozen men, all wearing masks, held guns on them.

"Who are you? And what do you want?"

"Names aren't no matter," Dingo replied. "And what I want is your watches. Your money. Anything that you might have stashed in that fancy wagon of yours."

"Outlaws!" Holz said.

"I'll handle this," Easton hissed.

"Think you're hot stuff, do you?" another outlaw asked. "Then handle this!" His massive fist snaked out and hit Easton, who fell backward in a daze. Easton kept his eye on him, trying to clear his head.

"Murdock, cut it out," the first outlaw said. "Pierce, you take some of the boys and take this fancy rig apart. The rest of you boys take whatever valuables you can find off these yahoos."

"Can I beat up on them some, too?" Murdock asked.

"Just do what you're told."

Holz was amazed to see Pierce and three others manually set the carriage upright again. Some of the papers that Easton had been working on fluttered to the ground through the open door.

"What's this?" Dingo demanded, kicking one of the sheets with a dirty boot. "You some kind of lawyers or something?"

"We're with the government," Easton said. He was still on the ground, rubbing his chin, trying to stand.

"Really, now." Dingo motioned to a smaller man. "Jessup, gather together some of these papers. It might prove interesting reading on some cold night." He laughed and pounded his fist on his knee.

"You can't do that! It's government property . . ."

Murdock ripped the watch from Easton's pocket and pushed him back to the ground. He pulled his gun and aimed it at Easton's head.

"Aren't we citizens?" Jessup asked calmly.

"Ah, well . . . convicted felons do lose certain rights . . ."

Jessup walked over and grabbed Easton's shirt collar. "What makes you think we're felons?"

"Ah, well . . ."

"Maybe you should apologize?"

"Of course. My mistake."

". . . and citizens with every right!" Holz finished.

From inside the carriage came a whoop, and one of the men came out holding a heavy bag. It clinked as he walked.

"We struck paydirt, boss!" the outlaw called out. "Looks like gold coin!"

Holz sighed. It had been his idea to bring along the gold to help with expenses. In the West, he knew, government IOUs weren't always considered acceptable currency. The loss of the gold could be a mark against him. Even so, he wasn't going to get himself killed over it, though he should at least make an effort.

"Anything else?" the leader of the band asked.

"You realize that this is a federal offense?" Holz asked.

"It makes me shiver in my boots!" Dingo laughed again. Holz said nothing more. "Now answer my question. Anything else of value here?"

"Nothing. You've cleaned us out."

"What about these yahoos? Should we shoot them?"

"Why waste bullets? We're miles from any-where. These tenderfoots won't last a day . . ."

Dingo stopped in midsentence as he seemed to listen to the air. Some said he could hear, see, and smell buffalo—and men—miles away. It made him one of the more dangerous buffalo hunters, and outlaws, working in that part of Texas.

"We're getting company," he announced. "I

don't know how many, but I think we've had enough fun for one day. Let's get out of here."

Murdock laughed and added, "You're right, Dingo! Let these greenhorns stew in their own fat!"

The others also guffawed as they quickly mounted and started to ride.

Holz knew Easton was sensitive about his weight, but was still surprised to see Easton unexpectedly stand and jump at the outlaw who made the comment about him being fat. He grabbed the outlaw's legs and tried to drag him from the saddle. The outlaw was apparently even more surprised. He looked down at his attacker, kicked, and lost his balance. He hit the ground with a thud. The other members of the gang didn't even bother to look back as they rode away.

"Now you've done it," the outlaw said. "I've had enough. I don't care what anybody says. I'm going to kill you."

His threat was interrupted by two bullets whizzing past him. One came from behind a rock—the driver who had been hurled from the vehicle. The other shot was from a tall man riding toward him on a fast horse.

Sam Two-Wolves knew better than to rush blindly into a fight. It was better to know the odds, know who was fighting and why. But this time Sam was angry and he didn't really care. He would be willing to face a den of rattlesnakes, if need be.

That what he found was a buffalo hunter was a stroke of good fortune.

Sam instantly sized up the situation. One man with a gun, pointed at another man, ready to shoot. A third man, bloodied, apparently helpless. The wrecked carriage. The dead rider motionless on the ground. It would be unusual for one man to do so much damage, so the other gang members would probably not be too far away.

Matt also realized the situation and called out, "I'll look for the others!"

Sam waved him away and didn't slow his horse for a second. He was willing to take his chances.

He was still too far away for a clear shot, but it was worth a try. He pulled his rifle and took aim. It was almost impossible to shoot a rifle accurately from a running horse, though Sam did better than most. The shot roared almost at the same time as another, fired by a man lying behind a rock. Both shots missed. The outlaw leaped behind the cover of the damaged carriage.

Sam shot three more times, not expecting to hit his target, but giving the two other men a chance to scurry to safety behind the rock. Sam slid off his horse and joined them.

"Got yourself in some kind of mess?" he asked conversationally.

"He called me fat!" Easton said, his face red. "That was so . . . so . . . unacceptable!"

Sam raised his eyebrows.

"I'm guessing you were also robbed and your lives threatened. Was that acceptable?"

The outlaw fired two shots blindly in the direction of Sam and the others. Sam returned the fire, but continued the discussion as if he didn't have a care in the world.

"I beg your pardon. My name is Carl Holz. This is Peter Easton. We're representatives of the government, on the way to Fort Concho to conduct some business . . ."

Easton quickly calmed down.

"Guess that was a crazy thing to do, attacking that man just because he called me a name. I could have been killed!"

"I understand. I'm kind of sensitive sometimes, myself. Problem is, I just shot the bastard. You never know."

"Are you all crazy?" the driver asked. "We've just been robbed, we're being shot at, and we're trapped! And you're all yapping your gums!"

"Not entirely correct!" Sam said. "We're not trapped at all. In fact, that fellow over there is the one in trouble. You stay here, and I'll take care of him."

Sam fired a shot and quickly reloaded. The outlaw returned the shots. Sam zigzagged across the short distance between the rock and the overturned wagon, dodging the bullets. The outlaw fired again, but this time the hammer fell on an empty chamber. Sam covered the remaining ground in a long leap.

Matt had kept up with Sam for most of the way to the place from which the shots had come. When he also saw the damage, but only one outlaw, he changed directions at the last minute. He had a feeling that other members of the gang were near and might unexpectedly return. His guess that they were still close-by was proven right when he spotted the dust cloud in the distance.

The gang was riding fast, though they did not have much of a head start. Even so, there wasn't much need for Matt to give chase. He was outnumbered and at this point had no reason to look for a fight. His intent now was to ensure that they did not turn around and surprise Sam in his skirmish with the lone bandit.

At one point the dust cloud paused, as if

the gang members were considering a return, but then the group continued on its way.

"No honor among thieves," Matt said to himself.

He watched the cloud grow smaller and then disappear before turning back to join up again with Sam.

Dingo and his gang had stopped briefly to rest and water the horses by a small stream. Dingo was looking at the back trail. Pierce also looked, but could see nothing. He looked up at Dingo with narrowed eyes and asked, "Aren't we going back for Murdock?"

"No."

"Why not? There can't be that many . . ."

"There's only two. I didn't see them, but that's my guess. But somehow I sense these two are different in some way. They could mean trouble for us, and I don't intend to look for trouble before its time. I don't intend to give up what we've gained just because that fool Murdock can't stay on a horse. Of course, if you want to go back, nobody's stopping you."

Pierce shrugged, and said, "He's no friend of mine. Way I look at it, he'll get what he deserves."

"I thought not."

"What if he talks?"

"If he gets any ideas about squealing, we'll just take him out. Simple solution to the problem. No more problem."

"What's the plan now?"

"We take the money we got from the buffalo hunt and the gold that those greenhorns so kindly provided to us and have ourselves some fun. There's some whiskey and women waiting for us."

"Fort Concho?"

"That's too close—no use taking chances. Let's head south. How does old Mexico sound to you?"

Sam landed on the outlaw. The force pushed him to the ground. He punched Sam in the chest with a closed fist, but Sam was young, strong, and muscular. He shrugged off the blow and rose to his feet.

"I don't know who you are, but you've gone and tangled with the wrong guy," the outlaw said. "Nobody messes with Mel Murdock."

"Yeah, I've heard those kind of threats before."

Murdock was heavier than Sam, but he was also slower. Sam ran toward Murdock, then pivoted at the last minute. Instead of the punch that Murdock expected, he found Sam beside him. Sam pounded the side of Murdock's head with a series of short, quick punches.

Murdock finally managed to dodge one of the blows and kick out viciously. Sam caught the foot and twisted, forcing Murdock to the ground.

In his anger, Sam was less cautious than he normally would have been. He twisted the leg until it felt as if it would give, but in a surprisingly quick move Murdock also twisted and kicked with his other leg. This again hit Sam in the chest, but with enough force that it pushed him back. Murdock, though limping, moved in with some more blows to Sam's stomach and chest, trying to wear Sam down.

In spite of Murdock's efforts, however, Sam was not getting tired. He just kept coming back for more, handing out more punishment than he received.

Sam directed his anger at Murdock, pummeling him with a series of short, hard blows to the stomach and head. Murdock evaded some of the punches, but not enough. His face had become covered with blood.

Finally, seeing he couldn't win, Murdock pulled out a long skinning knife and rushed. Sam was no stranger to knives, however, and sidestepped the attack. Sam sidestepped, grabbed the outlaw and threw him toward the wagon. He hit with a thud, but jumped up and ran again toward Sam.

A bullet whizzed past Sam and hit Murdock in the shoulder. He dropped his knife and fell backward against the wagon.

Leaning over the top of a rock was the driver, smoke still curling from his gun.

Three

Matt watched the distance for several minutes to make sure that the gang members did not return. He heard the gunshots from the area where Sam had been headed, but wasn't too concerned. Sam had been in many tough spots and knew how to handle himself. Matt almost felt sorry for the person who took pot-shots at Sam, considering the mood that his blood brother had been in all day.

By the time he returned to the scene, the fight was all but over. Sam and the outlaw were slugging it out, with Sam getting the better end of the deal, when the outlaw's charge with a skinning knife was halted with a single shot.

Sam was still standing, breathing hard, when Matt rode up and dismounted.

"The others got away," Matt said.

"That's not like you to let anybody get the best of you. You must be slipping."

"I suppose I could have covered the miles in seconds and brought them all in single-handedly, but I figured you'd need my assistance back here. I know how helpless you are when you get grumpy."

"I'm still not in a great mood . . . you want to see how helpless I am?"

Matt stepped back in mock horror.

"Oh, no! I never take advantage of a man when he's down!" Both men laughed, and Matt continued, "If you wanted to kill this fellow, your aim was off. Just goes to show you shouldn't shoot when you're in a bad mood!"

"I didn't shoot him," Sam said.

"I did," the driver said. He limped around the rock, then collapsed on the ground, holding his leg. "Damn him and his whole bunch. I'd like to shoot the whole lot of them."

Matt nodded toward the driver. Sam walked over to him while Matt checked out the outlaw.

Matt pulled his revolver and stepped cautiously toward the outlaw. His gun was on the ground. Matt picked it up, put it in his belt, and pulled down the outlaw's mask. He was a stranger to Matt, though he had seen many others like him in his travels. He was dressed like a buffalo hunter, but unlike some of the more respectable hunters, he was little more than a thug looking for easy money any way he could find it, and he wasn't too particular about where he found it. He was barely conscious. Matt ripped the bloodied shirt to expose the wound. It had been a clean shot. The outlaw would live.

Matt grabbed the man by his shirt, lifted him to his feet. He groaned as Matt shoved him toward the rock where the others were standing. Sam kneeled by the driver.

"Take it easy, pardner," Sam said, running his hand along the leg. "It's busted, sure enough, but it hasn't broken the skin. I think you'll live."

"The name's Guinn," the driver said. "I'm glad you fellows showed up when you did."

"You know who the gang was?

"I heard one of the fellows called Dingo. There's all kinds of thugs and outlaws running around this part of Texas these days, but only one Dingo Whaley. They got the jump on us. If you all hadn't showed up, I'm not sure they wouldn't have shot all of . . . *YEOOW!*"

His talk was interrupted by a scream of pain as Sam, without warning, twisted and pulled the leg to bring it back into alignment.

"Sorry, pardner, but it'll only hurt for a

while. We'll splint that leg and in a few weeks you'll be as good as new."

Matt noted the two other men standing near Sam. Both were wearing expensive suits, now torn and dirty. The shorter man's face was bloody and the larger man's face was bruised.

"This fellow on the ground called himself Mel Murdock," Sam said. "These two are Peter Easton and Carl Holz."

Matt handed Murdock's gun to Easton. "Watch Murdock. Shoot him if he tries anything. Holz, you let Sam look at that face. His bedside manner isn't much, but he can do some decent doctoring. I'm going to check out the damage to your coach."

As he expected, the damage was beyond repair. The horses were in poor shape. One of them had died instantly, as a result of a gunshot wound from a buffalo gun. Another had broken his neck. Two others had broken their hitches and gotten away. They would be fairly easy to find, because they would not have traveled too far from the scene. There would also be the horses that had been ridden by Murdock and the dead guard. It would be enough to at least get these greenhorns and the prisoner to the nearest law.

The vehicle was broken, in splinters. It was now little more than firewood. Three of the wheels had been busted off. What hadn't been destroyed in the wreck had been damaged by the outlaws, with huge gaps in the floor and the seats torn out. They had apparently been looking for something, probably money or gold. The two passengers stood out in this part of Texas like a sore thumb. They looked like they had money and would be easy pickings. It was a wonder they hadn't been attacked before now. Matt picked up some of the papers that littered the ground.

The guard was still spread out on the ground where he had fallen with a hole in his chest.

When Matt returned to the group, Holz's face had been patched up.

"It'll take a while to find the horses and bury the dead man," Matt reported. "Might as well forget about getting on the road again tonight. Hope you boys don't need to be someplace right away."

"Looks as if we have no choice," Easton said. "But I'm not complaining. We thank you for your help."

"You can show your appreciation by helping clean up this mess. You all bury that poor guy out there in the grass while Sam and I find your horses. We'll just camp out here for the night."

* * *

Sam found the outlaw's horse grazing near the camp. It was a fairly good horse, probably stolen from somewhere along the line. The dead guard's horse was found further away, in the general direction of San Angelo. He had the look of an army horse. Both still had their saddles on.

Matt found the two horses that had broken off from the team in the opposite direction. Unfortunately, one of them had a broken leg and could barely move. Matt never liked to put any animal out of its misery, especially a good horse, but sometimes there was no choice. He carefully removed the remaining harness, led the good horse a safe distance away, then unhitched the crippled animal.

"Sorry, fellow," he said, as he pulled the trigger.

The two blood brothers met at a predesignated spot with the recaptured horses. Sam saw that Matt was leading only one horse.

"The other one didn't make it?" he asked.

"Broken leg."

"Yeah. I heard the shot. Sorry."

"This hasn't turned out to be a real good day, has it?"

"You've got that right." Sam stepped down from his horse and crouched to the ground. Matt joined him. They talked in low tones, even though the nearest person was miles away.

"What do you want to do about those greenhorns?"

"I've already stuck my nose in their business, so that means we're already involved. They told me they had some business in San Angelo, which is the general area we're heading. They didn't say what their business was."

Matt pulled out the papers he had picked up from the ground.

"Looks like government business of some kind. Most of this looks like so much bull."

"That's news to you?"

"Come to think of it . . . no."

"Should we be reading government business?" Sam asked, grinning. "I think there may be a law against it, or something."

"Since when are you a stickler for the law?"

"Only when it serves the cause of justice."

"Now who's talking bull?"

"If it was good enough for Thomas Jefferson and Tom Payne, it's good enough for me."

"Sometimes I wish you have never gone to the university."

"An educated Indian can be a dangerous thing."

"A smart-ass Indian is even worse."

"You're just jealous of my articulate way of expressing myself."

Matt shuffled the papers, scanning them. "Well, this is interesting," he said. "Check this out."

Sam took the sheet. "Not much here, except for . . ." He grinned. "Well, I'll be damned. Josiah Finch. The old son of a gun. The other pages are missing, so I don't know what it means. Wonder if he's gotten himself in trouble again?"

"Don't Texas Rangers make their own law?" Matt asked innocently.

Sam laughed and handed the paper back.

"This could be interesting. I say, let's ride with these two for a while and see what develops."

While Holz and Easton finished digging the grave, Sam prepared the campfire, using wood from the wrecked carriage. When the two easterners returned to the camp after sundown, they were dirtied and blistered. Sam gave them credit, however, for completing the tough job without complaint. They sank wearily to the ground. Sam passed out beans and bacon that he had cooked for supper.

"Thank you again," Easton said. "You not only save our lives, you also feed us supper."

He ate hungrily. "Where are you all headed?"

"We're just drifters," Sam said. "We've just come back from up north, thought we'd see what this part of Texas looks like. Don't have any plans or any place we need to be."

"Carl and I were on the way to Fort Concho. I thought we were well-guarded, what with Guinn and the armed escort."

"His name was Rafferty," Guinn said, pushing himself to a sitting position. "He was a good man. And he was shot in cold blood. He didn't stand a chance."

"Did he have family?" Sam asked softly.

"No. His wife ran off with a snake-oil salesman years ago. He had some woman friends around the fort, if you know what I mean, but he never settled down. He worked as a hired guard for the army, the stagecoach line, wherever he was needed."

"A friend of yours?"

"We worked together off and on for lots of years."

"I'm sorry."

"At least we got one of his murderers. It'll be good to see him hang."

Guinn glanced over at Murdock, now tied and gagged with his own mask. That had been Guinn's idea, since the smelly mask was enough to make even a buffalo hunter sick.

It was small enough justice, but seemed fitting.

"Losing Rafferty and the services of Guinn is bad enough," Holz continued. "But we've also lost our transportation and our financial resources. We had some gold to use for expenses involved with our project. The outlaws took that as well."

"How much gold?" Matt asked.

"Not much. Maybe a thousand dollars."

"Some project!"

Holz shrugged.

"What about the gold?" Sam asked.

"We'll report the loss. Somebody will investigate."

"It'll all be spent by the time the paperwork's done," Sam suggested.

"Could be. That's the least of our worries now," Easton said. "I doubt that we'd make it the rest of the way on our own. We need some guides—somebody to help see us through. We've talked about it, and would like to hire you to ride with us the rest of the way to Fort Concho. We'll have to arrange for some additional money to be sent to us before you can be paid. But I can assure you that you'll be taken care of."

"What's the going rate these days for government service?" Matt asked. "I forget what the army pays, but I think the Texas Rangers pay about ten dollars per month."

"Oh, I can assure you that your pay will be much more than that!" Holz said. "This will be a special service that we will gladly pay you well for!"

"That's a mighty fine offer," Sam said. "But we don't hire out our guns. Not for any amount of money."

Easton's face fell in disappointment.

"But we will volunteer our services. We are civic-minded citizens, after all, and are willing to do our part."

"Excellent!"

"Matt and I will be glad to ride with you to Fort Concho and see that Murdock is placed safely in jail. We might even stick around for his hanging. Just keep in mind that we're not working for you, so don't get any fancy ideas just because you're with the government."

"You all are a rare breed of men. In fact, I'm not sure I've ever seen anybody jump in and so freely help others, when it puts your own lives in danger."

"Guess we've just got a soft spot in our hearts," Sam said.

"Or rocks in our heads," Matt added.

Four

Matt and Sam woke before dawn to prepare for the trip to Fort Concho. They already had the horses saddled and breakfast ready by the time that Holz and Easton moved slowly and painfully out of their blankets.

"I never expected *this,*" Easton said, his bones popping as he stretched.

"Why do you think the senator requested you to personally make this trip?" Holz asked. "He had an idea that west Texas might be as close to hell as you could find on this earth. And he thought you deserved it."

"I think he's gotten his money's worth. I'll be glad when this is all over." Easton said. Then he called to Matt, who was tending the cookfire, "How long to Fort Concho?"

"A good two or three days' ride, I think," he said. "Hope you two are used to horseback."

39

Easton groaned.

Sam walked up, leading the horses. He said, "We have a little problem."

"Another problem?" Easton asked. "I think we have more than our share."

"We have enough horses . . . but one of them doesn't have a saddle! Are you all going to draw straws to see who gets to ride bareback, or what?"

Matt stood up, grinning. "Maybe it'd be fair if they took turns. That way it'd give everybody a chance to be equally sore."

"No, that wouldn't work. Guinn has that broken leg, it wouldn't be fair to him. It'd probably be better just to let Holz and Easton share."

"Hey, wait a minute, Sam! You have the Indian blood. Maybe you should volunteer to ride bareback. You should be used to it!"

"Actually, to be modest, there's not a horse I couldn't ride, with or without a saddle, but in this case I think I'll pass. I'm kind of partial to my own mount."

Guinn hobbled up to the fire, poured himself a cup of coffee. "Is this discussion open to all?" he asked.

"Be our guest!"

"Why don't we hogtie our friend Mr. Murdock and sling him across the horse? It would certainly discourage any thought he might have of escaping."

"What a good idea!"

"And that way the rest of us could at least have saddled horses!"

As the group talked and laughed, Murdock glared at them over the mask tied around his mouth.

Matt said, "I suppose it'd only be fair to ask his opinion. This is a democracy, right?"

He stepped over to where the outlaw was stretched out and untied the gag. Immediately, Murdock said, "You monkey-assed good-for-nothing SOBs, I'd like to chop those smart-mouth tongues out of your mouth and—"

Matt's right fist moved in a blur; Murdock's head snapped back and his eyes glazed over.

"Majority rules," Matt said. "Murdock goes bareback. If he's as tough as he thinks he is, it won't bother him a bit."

Josiah Finch was seated in the simple chair across the desk from Col. Elvin Leeds, the commander in charge of Fort Concho. The two of them—Finch with the Texas Rangers and Leeds the United States Army—represented the only law-enforcement authorities on the frontier for hundreds of miles. It was a woefully inadequate force to combat Indians, outlaws, and Mexican bandits.

Finch was a small man—only about five feet four inches tall—and the gun at his hip seemed almost as big as he was. But Leeds had known Finch for a long time, first by reputation and then in person, and realized that few men in Texas were as fast with a gun as Finch nor as fearless when it came to a fight. Leeds had nothing but respect for the Ranger, but orders were orders.

"I appreciate you coming to me as soon as you got to town," Leeds said. "There's been a regular crime rampage recently, and I couldn't begin to tell you if there are organized gangs working or not. I suspect most of them are just mean SOBs out for what they can get. Hell, this town of San Angelo has been shot up so many times by buffalo hunters that I'm surprised there's anything left. I've ordered my men to stay clear of several of this town's watering holes—some of my men are so green I'm not sure how long they'd last. I've had dozens of crimes reported to me that I can't investigate because they're not within my jurisdiction, and many others I don't have the manpower to investigate."

"I'm on the trail of about three different gangs. The biggest is probably the Dingo Whaley gang. I don't know if they're going to pass through this way or not, but it seems reasonable. I figure I can at least hear something here."

"I'll work with you as much as I can. You know that." He reached into his desk, pulled out a sheaf of papers. "But I've been getting some heat from a lot of different directions. There's been several complaints about violation of state, federal, and international law. And you know what?"

Finch leaned back and crossed his hands behind his head. "I couldn't begin to guess."

"Your name is mentioned more than once in these complaints."

"Do tell!"

"I know when you're after those desperadoes it's tough to turn back at the border. Hell, we've all crossed the river plenty of times if we feel it's necessary. But for some reason they've singled you out for special attention!"

"It must be my winning personality."

"I'm just trying to warn you that some are trying to tighten things up down here. In fact, I've heard the rumor that Washington is sending down investigators to look into the situation."

Finch whistled. "Boy, that *is* rough!"

Leeds laughed. "Yeah, I agree. But my options this time are more limited. I don't have the manpower or the maneuvering room to give you much backup."

"Boy, since when have I needed much backup?"

Leeds laughed again. "You do have a point, Josiah. What do you say we go get a drink?"

"*Now* you're talking sense!"

It had been a long, hard ride, especially for Mel Murdock. He did learn, however, to keep his mouth shut, so that his foul gag was finally removed. Sam took no special care of the outlaw, but over the several days it took to reach San Angelo, the shoulder wound started to heal. Carl Holz and Peter Easton managed to salvage a change of clothes from the wrecked coach, but not much else. They decided not to change until they reached their destination, so by the time they arrived they did not seem near as dapper and well-to-do as when they started. Matt and Sam, on the other hand, were used to the saddle and the dusty frontier trails. They were hardly the worse for wear.

Easton looked at the small collection of adobe houses and businesses—most of them saloons—and asked, "I thought you said we were going to hit San Angelo this morning."

"This is it," Matt said.

"Home sweet home," Guinn said.

"There's nothing here!"

"This is a big city compared to a lot of places we've been," Sam said. "And over yonder is Fort Concho, I think. That's probably where your business will take you. After we drop off the prisoner, my business is going to be a good beer and a decent meal."

"I think I'd like a bath," Easton said.

"Good luck. You have a choice of baths in this town," Sam responded. "The North Concho or the South Concho rivers!" Still laughing, Sam turned to Guinn and asked, "You said you live here. Who's in charge of this place?"

"Last I heard, Colonel Leeds was the officer in charge, on a temporary basis until they can fill the position. His office is down there."

"Then, let's get it over with," Sam said. "I hear that beer calling my name."

Leeds was sitting at the desk in his office, signing some papers, when Matt, Sam, and the others walked in.

"Pardon me, sir, but you have nobody in front to announce us," Easton said.

The colonel looked up from his paperwork, his pen paused in midair. It had been a long time since he had seen such a motley crew. Matt and Sam looked like a pair of drifters, which were common enough in these parts. Their eyes twinkled good-naturedly, but the guns they wore low on their hips said they could also be dangerous. There was also a buffalo hunter with a bloodied and torn shirt and two greenhorns who were obviously the worse for wear. Jack Guinn brought up the rear.

"Hey, Jack. You I know. Who are your friends? And where's Rafferty? I was expecting you days ago . . ." Leeds stopped in mid-sentence, suddenly realizing what must have happened.

"We were attacked by outlaws," Guinn explained. "These two here are the ones Rafferty and me were hired to pick up and bring here. But we were attacked. Rafferty got hit first thing. He's buried out there somewhere on the trail. The outlaws would have probably killed the rest of us, if not for Matt and Sam here."

Leeds stood up from his desk, tapped his pen on his desk.

"Matt. Sam. Could you all be Matt Bodine and Sam Two-Wolves?"

"That's us," Matt said. Turning to Sam, he asked, "How do you think he guessed?"

"Maybe our fame has spread far and wide?"

"I've been hearing stories about you two," Leeds said. "You're not as famous yet as, say, General Grant or Sam Houston, but you're talked about. Matt, I talked to one fellow who

46

said you outdraw three men in . . . where was it . . . Colorado? And killed them all."

"Stories get exaggerated."

"And you, Sam. I've heard stories about how you can track a feather blown by the wind at midnight. Is that true?"

"Well, the stories about Matt *are* probably exaggerated, but not mine. That's true!"

"I've also heard about those little identical bands you all wear around your necks. Those three multicolored stones, strung together with rawhide. I won't ask what they represent, since it's none of my business. But I'd say it'd be hard to mistake you two."

"We'll take that as a compliment," Sam said. "But enough small talk. We'd like to get rid of this smelly trash here. Can you take him off our hands?"

Leeds walked over to Murdock, looked him up and down.

"And who are you?" Leeds asked. "Who are you working for?" Leeds asked.

"None of your damned business," the outlaw said.

"Would you like your mask back?" Matt asked.

The outlaw shut up. Guinn answered for him. "This is one of the gang that shot Rafferty. I heard him call one of the others Dingo. If that means anything."

"It could," Leeds replied. "I have a friend that would be quite interested in that information." He walked back to his desk. "How about the others? Any dead or wounded?"

"They were gone by the time we got there," Sam said.

"The others all got away," Guinn said. "Murdock's the only one that didn't get away. And he probably would have, if Easton hadn't jumped him."

Leeds took a closer look at Easton. He was overweight and didn't look like he could take on an outlaw. But one thing Leeds had learned in the army was that you never knew what people could do until they were faced with do-or-die situations. People always surprised you.

"This story sounds more fascinating by the minute. I think we can find a place to keep this fellow for a while. We have a circuit judge come through here every so often . . . I think he should be here again in a few weeks."

"Weeks! Dammit! I demand—"

"I wouldn't complain, if I were you," Leeds cautioned. "The longer it takes for the judge to get here, the more time you have until you're hanged."

Leeds called out the back door, "Corporal! Get me two men in here, pronto! And clear out one of the cells for a new resident!"

48

The colonel returned to his desk, sorted through a pile of papers. "Damned paperwork, that's all this job seems to be, sometimes. Wait, here it is." He read down the sheet. "So you're Peter Easton and Carl Holz. My orders are to show you every courtesy and to cooperate with you to the fullest extent. I have received little explanation of why you are here, though I suppose it has something to do with keeping international peace, or some such bull."

"First thing we need to do is to recuperate from our journey," Easton said. "I never thought I could be so sore in so many places. We also need to get word to our superiors in Washington about our status. Also to replenish our funds, since the outlaws got the money we had brought for expenses. After all that is accomplished, we will start to review some of your records and see if we can make contact with Mexican authorities to obtain their official version of events. You can be sure that our report will be fair and impartial."

"A report, eh? Very well. I'm sure that will have a major impact on the crime spree going on down here now." A corporal and two other men entered. Leeds ordered, "Take Murdock here to the blockade. We'll be holding him for a while until civil authorities can take appropriate action. Show Mr. Easton and Mr.

Holz to the guest lodging. They are representatives from Washington, D.C., so we will attempt to make their stay here as pleasant as possible."

As the other men left, Leeds continued, "Matt, Sam . . . would you join Jack Guinn and myself for a drink? I'd like to personally hear your story. I'll need to file a report, of course."

"Of course." Sam laughed. "Buy us a beer and we'll tell you all the stories you want."

"Buy us two beers, and some of the stories might even be true!" Matt added.

Five

The saloon from the outside was adobe, like most of the town. It was much nicer on the inside, with soft kerosene lighting on the walls and a long, polished wood bar along one side. It even had a mirror behind the bar and a painting of a seminude lady above the mirror. A piano player was playing a tune in another corner and the room was already filled with customers.

Matt and Sam noted that it was an unusual choice for Leeds, since there wasn't another officer in the place. In fact, there wasn't another army man present at all. There was the usual mixture of hard cases, cowboys, and drifters. Some of them were in a surly mood, but most seemed to just want to mind their own business, eating their meals and drinking their drinks.

"Hey, Rosie," Leeds said to a buxom woman brushing past him as they entered. "I've got some friends with me tonight. You got any of the good stuff left?"

She reached up, kissed him on the cheek. "For you, honey, I've always got the good stuff." She nodded to Guinn. "Good to see you, too, Jack. Hurt your leg?"

"Can't keep a good man down, you know."

"I see now why you like it here," Matt said.

"Rosie treats me right," Leeds answered. "She's a very special woman."

Leeds selected a small table in the rear as Rosie brought the drinks. Sam and Matt each took the glasses offered, but asked for beer the next round.

A whiskey glass suddenly flew overhead, shattering on the wall near Leeds. He ignored it.

"This is a nice, quiet place," Matt said.

"Quiet for this town. Wait a little while, and it'll get better."

"I can hardly wait."

"Now, tell me about this shoot-out you had. What do you know about the gang that robbed Holz and Easton?"

One of the girls brought over a tray of beers. She was a brunette, with a heart-shaped face and an hourglass figure. She set the glass in front of Sam, bending over deeply to do

52

so. Her dress was low-cut and left little to the imagination.

"Hey, handsome. You need anything, you call Mary. You got it?"

Sam, obviously embarrassed, said, "No, a beer is fine."

"Just keep me in mind."

Matt started laughing.

"I don't want to hear any more," Sam said. "Not after the way I've seen you get all stirred up about a saloon singer!"

"She was a singer who just happened to work in a saloon."

"Doesn't matter. This gal is probably interested in my good looks, and you're just jealous."

"Yeah. Maybe you look like a rich eastern tycoon!"

Matt looked up, but Mary ignored him, watching Sam like a hawk. Matt punched his blood brother on the shoulder, urging him to look. Sam punched back, a little harder than necessary, but Matt just continued laughing. Sam attempted to change the subject.

"To be honest, we didn't ask Murdock too many questions," he told Leeds. "We kept his mouth shut most of the time. Besides, we're new to the area and we're not the law. We brought the guy in, and you can ask him all the questions you want."

A cowboy stumbled past the table, tripped, and sent his glass of beer sailing across the room. He landed on the table, inches from Leeds.

"Damn, it's you, Leeds! I thought I told you to stay away from my girl!"

"I've told you before, Kurt, that Rosie is not your girl. I don't know why she wouldn't be interested in a low-life bum like you, and I don't intend to ask. Rosie is my girl. And even if she wasn't, it'll be a cold day in hell before I do anything you want. The only reason I don't pound your face in now is because you're drunk, which would make it too easy."

"Me and some of my friends have been talking. And we've decided that you can take your army brass and stick it—"

Leeds pushed the cowboy away. He slid from the table, fell to the floor. He crawled a few steps, stood, and left by the back door.

"A friend of yours?" Matt asked.

"I have lots of friends around this town. And I haven't even been here that long. Some people just don't like the uniform."

The piano player hit the keys a little harder, trying to be heard above the racket.

There were many saloons in San Angelo, and not even a Texas Ranger could visit all of them in one night. So Josiah Finch, in his usual direct fashion, started at the ones rumored to be the worst. He never drank much, just enough to make it look like he was drinking, though he never lost his edge. Though several would-be bullies approached him, something in his eyes made them continue to move on without saying a word. Finch in turn didn't say much, but listened a lot.

Word traveled fast in a small town, and within minutes of Matt and Sam's arrival in town with the prisoner, the news had spread rapidly. Finch heard about it while he was nursing his beer at the second saloon he had visited.

"I'll be damned," Finch thought. "What luck, with all the West to wander around in, I find those two boys right here in San Angelo!"

It didn't take much to determine that they were having a drink with Leeds at Rosie's. That didn't surprise the Ranger, since that was where the colonel usually spent his off-duty hours. It would be as good of a place as any to catch up on old times with the boys and compare stories. It was still early, however, and Finch wasn't in any hurry, so he ordered another beer and listened to the chatter going on around him.

One conversation in particular intrigued

him. It had something to do with rumors of a gold shipment coming in, but nobody knew when or where it would be stored. A logical choice would be the town's only bank, though it was not one of the most secure buildings around.

Rumors were only rumors, but sometimes rumors had elements of fact, and it could lead him to some of the gangs that he had been chasing.

Finch paid for the beer when it was set in front of him. It was weak and warm, but in this case the Ranger didn't mind because he was more interested in the talk than in the beer.

In old Mexico, just south of the border across the Rio Grande, Dingo Whaley was sipping tequila and rubbing against the señorita on his lap. He and his men still had plenty of money left, and were enjoying themselves in every way possible.

A knock on the door interrupted Dingo's pleasures, but he was getting tired of the woman, anyway. It was time for somebody new.

"Get on out of here," he said, slapping her on the rear. "I'll come back to you later."

The woman giggled, slipped her dress back

in place, and opened the door. Jessup smiled at her as she walked by.

"Interrupted something, boss?"

"Nothing important. There's more where that came from. Why aren't you enjoying yourself more?"

"I wasn't out hunting buffalo for as long as the rest of you. I remembered what a woman looked like. Besides, I've been thinking."

"You've got money, all the booze you could want, and all the woman you could want. What else is there to think about?"

"More money. More booze. More women. I'd hate to have all this dry up right when I get used to it. And, to be honest, I'm not real partial to the idea of more buffalo."

"You've got my attention. I can see your point and that you've been chewing on this for a while. Pour yourself a drink. Pull up a chair. I'm listening."

"It involves those guys we robbed. The ones that got Murdock. Something about that's been bugging me, so I finally got around to reading those papers I picked up."

"So?"

"So apparently there's been a real big stink brewing between the Mexicans and the States. Something about territorial jurisdiction and how Mexico is demanding the States stay off their soil."

"That's an old story."

"Right. But I'm not sure it's ever been to this point. I don't know much about this stuff, but I can figure the angles. So can you. Think about it for a minute. If those two clowns were sent down to investigate, maybe the government's serious about not allowing the law to give chase across the border. That means a smart operator could work out of Mexico and nobody in the States could touch them!"

"But about the Mexican federales . . ."

"How about a . . . partnership?"

"A partnership? With who?"

"The local authorities. Grease the wheels, so to speak, so that they will look the other way."

"Hmm . . . a cut of the profits in return for protection. Sounds . . . good."

"We could put those damned buffalo behind us . . . forever."

"Sounds good. We'll make plans tomorrow. For now, send that woman back in here. I'm suddenly feeling real enthused again."

At Rosie's, the crowd continued to grow and Mary continued her flirtation with Sam, though Sam was doing his best to ignore her. It wasn't that he didn't find her attractive, since she was quite a pretty woman. Rather, he didn't want to have to endure the endless kidding that Matt would throw at him. Even so, as the night wore on, his reserve grew less and he started to flirt back, much to the woman's delight.

It wasn't late yet—not even eleven P.M.— when Leeds stood up.

"Hate to leave good company, but morning comes mighty early in the army," he said. "I'll get back with you about the Murdock situation . . . oh, hell."

His eyes were fixed toward the bar. Sam looked up and also saw trouble brewing. Kurt, the drunk cowboy, had returned with several of his friends. They had cornered Rosie at the bar. Mary joined them when one of the men grabbed Rosie by the arm.

"Excuse me, fellows," Leeds said. "I need to help the girls."

He didn't bother to wait for an answer. He pushed his way through the crowd.

"I don't like the odds," Matt said. "I count six of them and only one of Leeds."

"That's not all," Guinn added. "Leeds didn't tell you everything about Kurt. He and his men have been involved in a petty-theft operation, trying to steal from the soldiers. Leeds called him on it, and Kurt swore revenge. Kurt may be drunk, but he and his friends are still dangerous."

"Then I say let's even up the odds a little," Sam said.

"Hell, you'd do anything to impress a woman, wouldn't you?" Matt said.

The piano player continued to pound the keys, the loud talk continued, but suddenly a change started to come over the room. The talk was a little more nervous. The music was a little more tinny.

Matt and Sam could hear the talk from the bar over the noise.

"I told you to get out of town, Kurt. You and your men. We all know that damned talk of yours about Rosie being your girl is just so much hogwash, trying to goad me into a fight. Well, you've succeeded. You touched Rosie, and that's it for me."

Kurt reached for his gun, when Sam called out, "You fight Leeds, you fight me and my friend. That evens up the odds some, don't you think?"

Kurt looked confused. "This isn't your fight. There's no need to get yourself killed. Just get lost and live for another day."

"I don't think so," Matt added. "Looks to me like you owe the girls here an apology. So just say your peace, and you walk out of here."

The bar suddenly started to go quiet. The ones near the bar started to slowly edge away, though the crowd made movement slow. The rest of the crowd also started to sense something wrong, though they didn't yet realize that a shoot-out was close.

"You want us to apologize to them? These dance-hall girls? These whores? You've got to be kidding!"

Kurt's hand suddenly slipped to his holster. As if on signal, the others also reached for their guns. Matt and Sam, however, were ready for it. Almost as one, both blood brothers shot, blazing fire and smoke.

The sound was deafening in the small space. Chaos suddenly filled the saloon. Tables and chairs were overturned, hitting the floor with loud crashes. Men and the dance-hall girls scrambled for cover. The piano player crouched under the keyboard.

Kurt and his men returned the fire, but for two of the men it was already too late. They fell lifeless to the floor, bullets through their hearts.

Kurt jumped behind the bar, shooting as he jumped. Leeds fired back, barely missing the mirror behind the bar.

Two other of Kurt's men headed for the door when they realized that they were outgunned. They made the mistake, however, of continuing to shoot. Matt and Sam continued to fire their guns, each bullet finding its mark. One man made it out the door—dead. The other was wounded as he stumbled from the room. A fifth man threw down his gun and held up his hands, which saved his life.

This left only Kurt, behind the bar. He shot wildly, the bullets barely missing some of the customers trying to hide underneath the tables. Leeds shot back from time to time, forcing Kurt to keep his head low and behind the counter.

Leeds moved cautiously, positioning himself to get a clear shot at where he thought Kurt would appear. For several seconds, the room was quiet, when Kurt finally stuck his head around the bar.

"Stop right there, Kurt," Leeds said.

Kurt ignored the order. He jumped up and shot three times at the sound of the colonel's voice. Leeds hit the floor and shot once, hitting the outlaw in the chest. He fell backward, landing on the bar.

For long minutes, the room remained quiet, filled with the smell of gunsmoke. Slowly, when everybody realized the shooting was over, they started to move again. Some of the men dragged the bodies from the saloon and the piano player picked up his stool.

"At least you all didn't damage that fine painting behind the bar," a familiar voice from the corner said.

Matt and Sam turned almost as one and said, "Josiah Finch!"

The Ranger was sitting at the only table that had not been overturned, drinking a beer, acting as if nothing at all out of the ordinary had just happened.

"I see you boys *still* can't stay out of mischief, can you?" he asked.

Six

The three men were trying to work quietly, but it was difficult in the darkness. Armed with pry bars, they were making good progress through the back wall of the small building that served as a bank in San Angelo. A small attempt had been made at security, adding some planks to the adobe, but it was not enough to keep out somebody determined to get in.

"I still ain't sure this is a good idea, Fisk," one of the men said.

"It's just a small hole; nobody should notice it in the dark. We'll get inside, blow the safe, and be out of here before anybody can stop us. See, Ben's already inside. Stop worrying, Tom."

All three of the men were dressed in patched jeans and faded shirts. Their faces were unshaven and they smelled of too many bars and not enough work. Like many in the little cowtowns of the West, they were drifters looking to pick up some easy money in whatever ways they could. They had also heard the talk of a gold shipment.

"I can't help but worry," Tom answered. "This seems like a half-baked idea to me. We don't even know how much money is here. What if something goes wrong? And what will Leeds do when we take his payroll? You saw what he and his friends did at Rosie's a little while ago."

"That was personal. If it was army business, he'd still be filing reports before he'd even think about coming after us."

"I don't know. He didn't go by the book with Kurt, even before he started in on Rosie. He may be career army, but I don't know."

"Next thing you'll be worrying about those two drifters that helped Leeds."

"Yeah. I am."

"Forget it. It's not like they're Texas Rangers or anything. Let's get inside. And get this business taken care of."

"Pull up some chairs, boys," Finch continued. "If you can keep out of trouble long enough, that is."

"Of all the people to run into!" Matt said. "We haven't seen you in ages!"

"I heard you two were in town, decided to look you up."

"We've only been here a few hours," Sam said. "You work fast."

"Seems to be a lesson I taught you all, as well." The Ranger nodded his head at Mary. "Sam, think your friend could bring us some fresh drinks? Hell, don't look so surprised. It doesn't take a genius to see the way she looks at you."

At the bar, Rosie was busy dusting off Leeds, making sure he wasn't hurt. The colonel was obviously enjoying the attention. Mary saw the men talking, and didn't waste a second. She brought a new tray of beers over and set them on the table. Finch winked at her, but she ignored him to look at Sam.

"You were very brave, a few minutes ago. Not many men would have fought for me that way. Thanks." She reached out, gently touched Sam's shoulder. He patted her hand slightly, and she smiled as she turned back to the bar.

"Nice looking woman, Sam. Maybe you could teach this old Ranger a few tricks?"

"Some things just come natural."

"I wouldn't look to Sam for lessons, any-

66

way," Matt said. "He's got lousy taste in women. He never listens to my advice."

Finch shook his head, but continued to smile. "You boys never change, do you? Damned glad to see it."

Matt leaned back, sipped his fresh beer. "What brings you to San Angelo, Josiah?"

"I'll be direct with you boys, like I always have. As you know, we've been having a flood of bank robberies, stage holdups, and wholesale rustling sweeping into the Texas countryside. The Rangers are spread too damned thin. I myself am investigating the involvement of at least three gangs."

"And you have evidence that suggests they're working out of this area?"

"Nope. Not even a shred."

Matt looked puzzled as he placed his beer on the table. "Then why San Angelo?"

"Why not? It's a gathering spot for buffalo hunters and others of that type. It's got a stage line running through it. It's relatively near the Mexican border. It seems a logical spot. But there's something even more important."

Sam nodded his head wisely. He knew what was coming. But Matt asked, "And what is that?"

"A hunch. Something told me to show up here. So here I am. And here you are."

"And here we are?"

"Hell, yes. I was hoping to run into you boys. I'll lay my cards on the table, no playing games. The Rangers need more manpower, but it's damned hard to find the kind of men we need who are willing to work for what we pay. So you two are just the ticket. You've got the guts, the gumption, and the smarts. You can shoot. You can fight. You can track. And you work cheap. I'll bet you the next round of beers that you brought that Murdock character in and served as bodyguards for these political types just out of the goodness of your hearts."

"Remind me never to play poker with you, Josiah."

"Keep that in mind, Sam. I'd clean you out before the evening was half over. But that's neither here nor there."

"Get to the point, Josiah."

"I'm offering you two a job. How'd you like to join up with the Texas Rangers?"

Fisk easily slipped through the opening near the ground. Tom had a little more difficulty since he was bigger than Fisk and Ben.

"Dammit, you should have made this hole bigger."

"You should have skipped a few meals."

"Shut up and help me in."

Ben walked over and saw the situation. "Why don't you clowns stop fooling around?"

"Tom's stuck."

"Not stuck. Just having a little difficulty."

"At this rate, we'll never get this bank robbed. We'll help you through. Come on, take hold."

The two men standing over Tom reached down, each taking one of his arms, and dragged him through the rest of the way. Part of his shirt caught on the rough opening and ripped.

"Damn, that was my good shirt!"

"Forget it. After tonight, you can buy a dozen new shirts."

Ben stepped back over to the safe. "Remember, here's the plan. I set the powder in the safe and the door. They'll blow at the same time. Each of us grabs as much as we can handle. We go for the gold, but we could use the paper, too."

"How much gold would there be for the army payroll?"

Fisk scratched his head. "Come to think of it, I don't rightly know. The only gold I've ever managed to get hold of disappeared so damned fast I couldn't get a feel for it. I've seen some of the prospectors up in Colorado bring it in. I imagine it'd be at least one bag each."

Tom whistled. "Damn!"

"You said it. We'll have it easy then. No doubt of that!"

Ben continued, "Where were we? Oh, yeah. We get the gold and some paper. Then we skip out through the hole in the wall that the explosion makes."

"How much time you figure we have?" Tom asked.

"It'll be at least several minutes before anybody can react. And I can't imagine too many rushing into a burning building and possibly a bunch of bullets. It'll be enough time."

"Still say we should have practiced it," Tom said.

"And when would we do that? Hell, even those fools working for Leeds would know something was up if they saw us jumping around practicing a damned bank robbery!"

"The horses are tied out back," Ben concluded. "We'll meet at the old campsite by the North River. Understand?"

The other two nodded their heads.

"This will be the easiest money we ever made," Fisk said. "Don't know why we never thought of it before."

Ben started to work on the safe.

* * *

Matt and Sam laughed for about five minutes. They pounded their knees, leaned back in their chairs, and rolled their heads. Through it all, Josiah Finch calmly sat back in his chair, drinking his beer.

Finally, calming down, Matt asked, "Are you serious? Sam and I would be terrible Rangers. We do things our way. We don't take orders. When we start something, we don't stop until we do what we set out to do, and whoever gets in our way be damned."

"Exactly," Josiah agreed.

Matt looked at Sam. "He's serious."

"You're right. He is serious."

Colonel Leeds walked slowly over to the table, his arm around Rosie.

"Quite a party you're having, Josiah."

"These boys have a good time wherever they go. I suppose you know Matt Bodine and Sam Two-Wolves."

"Oh, yes. We've met. These boys cut a wide path wherever they walk. They brought in that outlaw, Murdock, earlier today. Good men. And good company." Rosie tugged at his sleeve, but he continued to talk. "By the way, Josiah, something you might be interested in. Guinn says that Murdock called one of the gang members Dingo."

"Well, that is *real* interesting," Finch said. "I'll pay that boy a visit. With your permission, of course."

"Be my guest." Rosie tugged at his sleeve again. "Right now, however, that shoot-out took a lot out of me. Rosie is going to see me home. I need to get up early tomorrow and prepare my report about this incident tonight."

"By all means!" Josiah winked. "You need your beauty sleep. But before you get away, I'll ask your advice. What do you think about Matt and Sam joining the Rangers?"

Leeds paused, examined the two blood brothers again, and pronounced, "They'd make better Rangers than they would soldiers."

"A diplomatic answer if I ever heard one!" Sam said.

Leeds sighed. "I'll need all the diplomacy I can get with these two easterners underfoot tomorrow. But it's all part of the job, I suppose. Good night, gents."

After Leeds left, Finch said, "He's a good man. A little too much spit and polish for my taste, but not a bad sort. Now, let's get back to business. I'm not asking you to make a career of the Rangers. Just join my company until I can wrap up some of my investigations.

I'd be willing to bet that we could put a lid on some of this crime spree here in Texas."

"Keep talking."

"Look at it this way. Even the federal boys need you. Things are getting pretty bad when our own government representatives are attacked in broad daylight by a gang of outlaws!"

"You have a point. But we may not be *that* patriotic."

"You might want to consider this. You heard Leeds. This may be the bunch I've been after for quite some time—a gang led by a mean SOB named Dingo Whaley. I'm hoping to get some hard evidence against them. Since you've already tangled with them, and brought in Murdock, you all would be a natural choice to help continue with the investigation."

"Murdock looked like a buffalo hunter," Sam said. "That mean anything?"

"The Whaley gang has been known to make some legitimate money as buffalo hunters. Pardon me, Sam. If you can consider such a thing as legitimate."

"Then count me in," Sam said. "I'll go after them just for the fun of it."

"You've convinced Sam. You still need to convince me."

"OK, Matt. I'll give you something else to consider, as well. I know you boys. I know the kind of mischief you can get into. While you're in Texas, I'd just as soon keep an eye on you, and it'd be easier if you're working for me."

Matt laughed again. "You silver-tongued devil! At least you're honest! It'd be interesting to see you try to keep an eye on us!"

Sam also laughed, but added, "If anybody could do it, Josiah would be the man!"

"You've got me," Matt relented. "You can count me in, as well. Just keep in mind that you owe us one!"

Inside the small bank building, Fisk asked, "What's taking so long?"

"It's hard to see in this dark. Get too much powder, and I'll blow this place sky high. Too little, and it wouldn't blow out a gnat. It's delicate work."

"Just get to it."

"Fine. You got a match?"

"Ummm . . ."

"You didn't bring a match?"

Tom spoke up, "I got one."

Ben took it, and said sarcastically, "I hope somebody remembered to put the horses out back."

"I took care of that," Fisk said. "That was my job. Matches were *your* job."

Ben struck the match without another

74

word, lit the fuses, and dived for cover with the other two. The fuses spluttered and sparked for what seemed like minutes, and then two explosions rocked the building. The robbers ignored the adobe, wood splinters, and dust raining down on them. Any disagreements they may have had were forgotten as the safe door was jerked open.

"Is that the gold?" Tom asked. Inside were only a few small bags and some currency tied together in bundles. "It don't look like much."

"I don't know," Fisk Yelled back. "Just grab as much as you can, whatever you can. Then let's get out of here. Remember, we'll meet on the river!"

Josiah Finch stood, reached out, and shook hands with Sam and then with Matt.

"I'm glad you decided to see things my way," Finch said. "It'll be good having you boys work with me!"

"When are you going to swear us in?" Sam asked.

"Well, let's see. We could finish our beer first, or maybe two beers . . ."

"Not in any hurry, are you?"

"You know me. No need to beat around the bush."

Explosions suddenly were heard over the noisy crowd. Most of the customers in the saloon either didn't hear the sound or ignored it. Finch and his new recruits, however, jumped to attention.

"I've changed my mind. How about being sworn right now?" the Ranger asked. "Raise your right hands. Do you swear to do your damndest to uphold the laws of the State of Texas and so on and so forth? In that case, boys, you all are Texas Rangers." He reached into his pocket, pulled out two badges, and handed them to Matt and Sam. They pinned the metal to their shirts. "Now, let's see what the hell is going on!"

Seven

The robbers worked quickly inside the small building. The gold and stacks of paper were stuffed in the bags and the three men left through the hole in the wall. All three had their guns drawn, but surprisingly few people were on the street, even after the explosion.

Fisk was the first to reach his horse. He spurred it out of town, almost running down a drunk cowboy leaving one of the bars. Ben and Tom were almost as quick, though they took off in two other directions.

Tom's path took him past the building where Leeds lived. He was hastily coming through the door, pulling on his pants. Tom took a shot at him, just for the fun of it. A shot came from behind him. Both shots missed, though Tom heard the bullet whiz past his ear. He spurred his horse to even more speed as he looked back and saw the small Texas Ranger, Josiah Finch, holding a smoking gun. His shot had come mighty close for the Ranger to be so far away, and Tom was going to take no further chances.

The outlaw didn't bother to shoot back. All he wanted now was to make his escape. He felt the weight of the bag against his leg, felt the horse under him, and made good time out of town. He had been involved in all kinds of petty crimes in his life, and had spent quite a bit of time in jail because of them. This was the first time that he had possibly made any real money, even though they hadn't gotten as much gold as Fisk had promised. He had no idea how much gold was actually in the bag.

Behind him, the town was starting to come alive, but by then he was a good mile outside town and quickly putting more distance between them. After another two miles, he slowed his horse to a walk and directed his horse off the main trail. He wondered if anybody would give chase, and when. He thought about covering his trail, and wondered if the other two robbers also would. But could anybody track in the dry Texas soil? He had never thought about it before. The other two had seemed so certain that the plan would work. He had thought so too—for a while. Now he had an awful lot of questions, but the deed had been done. There would be no turning back.

Tom was now traveling by starlight and came to a small hill. Faint trails led to either side of it. One trail led to the agreed-upon meeting place. The other trail led to the east, and then south in a roundabout way, perhaps to Mexico. He had never been to Mexico and wondered what it would be like. The bag now seemed comfortable against his leg. He wondered what he would gain by meeting with the other two, as planned. Perhaps they were being followed by Leeds or his men. Would they have more or less in their bags than Tom had in his? What would happen if he just kept riding?

The horse waited patiently as the outlaw thought about his options. He got off the horse and opened the bag. It was too dark to make out any details of the bag's contents. He looked behind him. It was still quiet. He crouched down and started a very small fire, just enough to cast some light to examine the gold and paper.

The amount of gold was disappointingly small—only about $300 worth of gold coins. He had risked his life for that? He untied the bundles of paper, and was even more disappointed. It was some currency, but primarily

IOUs from the army. They would be virtually worthless to anybody but the bank, since nobody else could possibly collect on those debts.

Obviously, Fisk had made a mistake. There was no payroll at the bank. Maybe there never would be. Tom doubted if Fisk or Ben had done much better. Still, $300 was enough for some whiskey and a poker game. Maybe it would be enough money to get him south of the border. He had heard that some outlaw gangs were working out of Mexico. Maybe he could join up with them.

He decided it would be better to cut his losses and run.

Angrily, he threw the paper on the small fire. He cursed, for the paper caused the small flame to flare up. He kicked dirt at it and hoped that nobody had caught sight of the fire.

Matt and Sam lowered their hands and instinctively checked the guns in their holsters. They pushed through the crowd after Finch, who was already outside the door. Some of the customers started to push back, until they saw who was doing the pushing. After seeing Matt and Sam beat the outlaws in a shoot-out earlier in the evening, nobody was now willing to take them on.

"Is it customary to put your new Rangers to work so quickly after being sworn in?" Matt yelled out.

"Nope. Usually we let them finish their drinks. For you boys, I made the exception!"

They got to the street in time to see one of the outlaws almost run down a cowboy. Two others were riding away in different directions. One of the outlaws took a shot at Leeds as he passed. Josiah pulled his big gun and took a shot. The outlaw kept riding.

"Damn, missed!" Finch said.

"If you hit him, it would have been a lucky shot at this distance," Matt said.

"Lucky for you," Sam said. "Not for Josiah."

"Thanks, Sam. Makes me glad I hired you. I'll have to talk with Matt one of these days about his skepticism."

A crowd had now started to form, so Finch holstered his gun again.

Sam said, "They went different directions. I think I can track—"

"You're a damned fine tracker, Sam, but let's not go off half-cocked. Let's take a look at the damage and see what's going on."

Leeds had on his pants and a shirt by the time Finch and his new recruits had made it to the building. Leeds paused long enough to pull another man from the crowd. Finch looked over the damaged building with an experienced eye.

"Didn't expect to see you again so soon, Josiah," Leeds said. "I had better things planned for my time."

"Bet you did. She'll wait. Is that the banker?"

The other man nodded. "The name's Barney Cooper. I represent the bank association."

"We'll talk in a minute." Finch turned to Matt and Sam. "Clear out these rubbernecks, will you? I have some questions for our friends here. Let's go inside what's left of the building."

Fisk had a fast horse and made good time. He arrived at the river just hours after the robbery. The other two hadn't shown up yet. He opened his bag, and was also disappointed at how little gold there was. It had seemed like a good plan, but that had been after several drinks. Now, he was sobering up, and the full realization hit him that he had just robbed a bank almost across the street from an army post. That was not the smartest thing he had ever done, though enough gold would have made the risk worthwhile. The gold in his bag wasn't enough. He had stuck his neck out for almost nothing.

He put the money back in the bag and made himself comfortable, pulling a bottle out of his saddlebags. He took a sip and thought about the situation. The more he drank, the more angry he got about the gold. Was it his fault that the shipment wasn't at the bank like it was supposed to be? Why should he have to suffer? The other two clowns almost messed up the robbery, in any case. Did they really deserve equal shares? Maybe, if he could combine his gold with the other two men's . . . and keep it for himself . . .

Fisk took another sip of whiskey and did some mental calculations. Unless they had a whole lot more then he did, it still wouldn't make him rich, but it would make him feel better about the job. After a few more drinks, he had his plan. He would simply take their gold for himself. They could have the paper money if they wanted it.

He hid, waiting for the other two to show up.

Finch was sitting in the chair behind the banker's desk in what was left of Cooper's office, forcing the banker to stand. Leeds was sitting on the edge of the desk. Matt and Sam were near the door.

"You've got a pretty small operation here," Finch observed.

"We've just gotten started. We plan to grow with the town."

"Looks like the robbers blew the safe. What was in it?"

"Not much. We don't have much on hand. Some gold. Some paper. Some currency. Some markers."

"Not hardly enough to make all this trouble worthwhile?" Finch said.

"Apparently it was to the robbers."

Finch leaned forward, put his elbows on the desk. "I'll be straight with you. It's no secret that a big shipment of gold is coming in for the army payroll. If I heard the rumor, so did others, but they didn't listen as closely as I did and must have thought it had already arrived and was kept in the bank. Am I right?"

"Mmmm . . ." Cooper said.

Leeds spoke up, "That's a good guess, Josiah. I'll make sure that the actual shipment is in a much more secure place than this bank."

"I'm sure you will. But what concerns me is that another try will be made when the gold actually gets here. We need to take that into account. Me and the boys will work with you on that. In the meantime, I reckon we'll go after the yahoos that robbed Cooper's bank."

"I'm glad you see fit to get back my money," Cooper said.

"Oh, that's not the crime I'm concerned about," Finch drawled.

"Really?"

"I'm more concerned about the crime of disturbing our peace. I was having a good time drinking with these boys until they blew your building to pieces!"

Ben wasn't real satisfied with his work. The holes in the buildings were too big, but he had claimed to be an expert, and they did the job. The safe was open, they had gotten away, and the loot was in the bags.

He had grabbed as much of the gold as he could find. When added to that taken by Tom and Fisk, it would probably total a decent amount. He doubted if anybody would give chase. He knew from talk around town that there was really no law to speak of except for the army and the one Ranger in town, and they would be too busy with other problems to go after a few small robbers.

Ben was not that familiar with the area, and had to go slowly over the rough terrain. Several times he almost got lost, until he found his way again. The robbers had not agreed upon a time to meet, which was just as well, since Ben was making such poor progress.

It was getting near morning when he finally reached the wide spot near the river where the robbers were to meet. He moved cautiously, suspicious when he saw no sign of life. Where were Fisk and Tom?

Ben's horse moved slowly toward the river. He stopped at the water's edge to allow the horse to drink. The outlaw stepped down, dropped the reins, and sat on a dry spot away from the water. Apparently he was the first to arrive, in spite of his delay.

He opened the bag and started to count when he heard the other rider.

"So you finally made it, Ben?"

"That you, Fisk?"

"Been waiting for you."

"Then why are you hiding? Come on out!"

"You got the gold?"

Ben held up the bag. "Right here! I was just getting ready to count it!"

Fisk stepped out from behind a bush, holding a gun at Ben's stomach.

"Let's count it together."

Ben realized that Fisk had been drinking. Sure, they'd had a few drinks in town while they planned the robbery. If they hadn't, they might not have had the courage to try it. But why would he drink now that they had gotten safely away?

Something in Fisk's voice made Ben tense up, but he was on the wrong end of a gun and could do nothing now except to follow orders.

Leeds followed the Rangers outside. "I can get some men together to help you hunt these fellows down," he said. "I don't want them running loose when the gold really gets here."

"I wouldn't worry too much about these robbers," Matt said. "I doubt if they could plan or carry out a bigger job than this."

"That's true," Finch agreed. "I'm more concerned about Murdock's friends—the Whaley gang. And since one of their men is your prisoner, that makes me even more nervous. On the other hand, it might work out for the best, since I've been trying to get some evidence on them for a long time. We might be able to use all this to our advantage."

"You've got a plan, Josiah?" Leeds asked.

"We'll take care of that when the time comes. For now, these boys are anxious to be on the trail. So am I, for that matter. Thanks for offering us the use of your men, but I think they'd just get in the way. We can make better time on our own. And we won't need any help bringing in these jokers. We'll take care of it. You get back to that unfinished business."

Finch slapped Leeds on the back, turned to Matt and Sam.

"Each of you take a man. They'll probably meet up someplace close to town. I have some ideas about where they might meet. I have a little business to take care of here, then I'll find you two. Between the three of us, we'll have these fellows brought in by morning and we can start thinking about more serious business."

"Like breakfast?" Sam asked.

"You learn fast." Finch laughed.

Eight

Matt saddled quickly and pointed his horse in the direction that Tom, the outlaw who had shot at Leeds, had gone. It was still dark, but would soon be dawn. There was already enough light he could make his way. He wondered why Josiah had taken so long to go after the outlaws who robbed the bank, but the Ranger was older and more experienced and had the trust of Matt and Sam like few other men had. So if Josiah felt there was no need to hurry, Matt would go along with the decision.

A light was burning in the colonel's quarters as Matt rode by. Maybe Leeds was already working? "Spit and polish" was the way that Josiah described the colonel; apparently he was right. Matt decided that he never wanted that kind of job: too much paperwork. He predicted, however, that Leeds would go far in his army career, if he didn't step on the wrong toes.

Matt didn't ride slowly, but neither did he hurry. He was following the main road out of town, keeping his eyes open. The dirt road turned into a wide path. On each side was scrub grass and mesquite. Matt preferred more grass and trees than this land had to offer, but he was glad to see this part of the country. He was young and had plenty of time to return home.

If he didn't get killed first. He and Sam had been in all kinds of fights in their wanderings, and so far he had managed to come out on top. He wasn't concerned about the outlaw he was now chasing, nor the Whaley gang that Finch was interested in. Matt figured he would face them down just as he had dozens of others before. It would not be easy, but he would be ready for whatever came his way.

He noticed a few small marks in the dirt on the right of the trail. It was an even smaller path. The marks and the path could barely be seen, and would have been missed if he hadn't been looking for them. He was not near the tracker that Sam was, but his blood brother had shown him a few tricks and Matt did a fair job. There was no guarantee that this was the outlaw's trail, though the marks looked fresh and he had a hunch it would be. He turned his horse to follow the faint trail.

As Matt rode, he had to smile at the unexpected turn that his and Sam's life had taken. Both were now sworn-in Texas Rangers! Matt wasn't sure what that really meant, except that they would now have a duty to nose into trouble as legally appointed peace officers instead of stumbling into trouble as private citizens. Matt and Sam never hesitated to fight or shoot when the occasion demanded, and the Rangers knew few limits when it came time to bringing in the men they were after or handing out rough frontier justice. He figured they would fit in just fine for as long as they remained on the force. It had been a spur-of-the-moment decision, but Matt and Sam would do the best jobs as Rangers that they knew how to do.

At the moment, that meant bringing in the outlaws.

The sky started to lighten in the east. Gentle rolling hills could now be seen in the distance, still in shadows. Matt still saw the faint trail. Apparently the outlaw was moving fast, not caring if he left telltale marks in the soil.

The trail led to a small hill. The path split in two, going in opposite directions. The ground here was more rocky, making tracks more difficult to see. Sam probably could have figured it out, but Matt was temporarily stumped. He could make a guess and follow one of the forks until he found some more sign, but that could take too long. He fully intended to bring in his man before breakfast—just to see the look on Finch's face!

Matt urged his horse up the small incline. The land here was relatively flat, and even this little hill gave him a broad view of the surrounding area. He didn't really expect to find anything but hoped he might get lucky. He slowly scanned the hills in the distance. At first he saw nothing. As he looked again, however, he thought he saw a tiny flicker to his right. It was bright for an instant, and then was gone. Perhaps it was nothing, but Matt decided to take the gamble. He rode down the hill to take the path on the right.

Josiah Finch stepped boldly into the building that served as a jail in San Angelo. It was really part of the fort and manned by soldiers, constructed of rock with bars over the windows and doors, but it had also held its share of civilian prisoners. This night it held Mel Murdock. The soldier guarding the prisoner stood and blocked the door leading back to the cells.

"Sir?"

"I'm here to talk with the prisoner," Finch said.

"That is highly irregular."

"Then check with Leeds," Finch snapped. "Last I saw, he was with Rosie and headed for home. If you don't trust me, feel free to check with him. I'm sure he won't mind being interrupted."

The soldier gulped.

"It's not a matter of trust, sir. I was just told to guard the prisoner . . ."

"I'm a captain in the Texas Rangers. That gives me authority. Are you going to step aside, or do I have to get nasty?"

Though Finch was a small man, his tone of voice left no doubt as to his intentions. The soldier moved to one side, handing the cell keys to Finch as he passed.

"If you don't mind, I will continue to stand guard here," the soldier said.

"Do your duty."

Murdock was asleep on his bunk when Finch entered. The key in the lock was loud in the small space, waking the outlaw. He blinked several times, but Finch gave him no time to react. The Ranger reached down and pulled the outlaw up by his shirt and said, "The name's Josiah Finch. Texas Ranger. You and I are going to have a little talk."

"I have nothing to say."

Finch pushed Murdock down on the bunk and leaned against the wall opposite him.

"We have hard evidence that you killed that driver back on the trail. You'll probably hang for that."

"Not a chance. There's no evidence I pulled the trigger. There were lots of us. We wore masks. Nobody could identify us."

"It'll be enough for a Texas judge and jury. You know that. You're already as good as hanged. Hell, we might even hang you before the judge gets here. Save the state the cost of a trial."

"That'll never happen. They'll break me out, first—" Murdock caught himself and stopped in midsentence.

"Just who are 'they'? Who do you work for?"

"I don't work for anybody."

Finch drawled, "I know better. You're one of Dingo Whaley's gang. We could probably work a deal if you tell me what I need to know. Where are they now? What are their plans? If you lead me to them, I might be able to keep your neck out of a noose."

Murdock suddenly looked nervous. He said, "Do I look stupid? They'd kill me if they even thought I had turned on . . . I mean, if I worked for somebody else, they wouldn't like it."

"I know Whaley's reputation. I think you just confirmed what I thought I already knew. You're one of Whaley's gang. That's all I need to know. For now."

"Blow it off, old man. Peddle it elsewhere."

"You might be surprised where I peddle it," Finch said.

He left the cell, closed it with a loud clang. The soldier was waiting for him.

"Where are you headed for now, sir? Do you have a message for the colonel?"

"I'm off to join two of my fellow Rangers. With any luck, I'll find them and be back before Leeds is out of bed in the morning."

Sam was not making real good time in the search for his man. The trail was easy to follow, but the outlaw seemed to wander around. At first, Sam thought the outlaw was trying to confuse the trail, but quickly decided he was probably just lost. So all Sam could do was continue to follow the trail to see where it led. He would hate to let Matt get his prisoner and be back in town first, since he would gloat and be generally insufferable. Sam also knew patience, however, and shrugged off his frustration as he followed the robber he was after.

As Sam rode, he thought about the situation he now found himself in. Sam's mother had been a white woman. He had been educated in an eastern university. Most of the time, he lived quite well in a white man's world. Even so, he still had Cheyenne blood in him. It was tribes other than the Cheyenne who were contributing to many of the problems being confronted by the Texas Rangers, but it was still Indian blood running in his veins. Now, he had been sworn in as a Ranger. He shook his head at the odd turns that life sometimes took.

The morning sun was starting to shine faintly from behind the hills. Sam could smell the faint odors of a river. The man he was following had apparently found his way, for his path for a while made a straight line for the river, only to veer off again. This time, Sam didn't follow the tracks because he found a second set of tracks, also leading to the river. This could be the place where the robbers would meet—if the outlaw he was following ever found his way. Sam dismounted to continue on foot.

He didn't have far to travel. He almost stumbled upon a man stretched out on the ground, watching the river, taking sips from a small bottle. He had his gun on the ground beside him within easy reach. Sam also fell to the ground, unnoticed by the outlaw. He remained motionless for long minutes. His patience was awarded when a third man rode onto a wide spot near the river. He rode hesitantly, then dismounted and looked around expectantly, holding a bag in his hand that he started to open.

The outlaw on the ground capped his bottle, picked up his gun, and stepped out from behind the bush where he was hiding, pointing his gun at the other man's stomach.

Sam pulled his own gun and inched closer so that he could hear the talk.

"Sure, Fisk. We'll count it together."

"You bet we will. Just hand me the bag." The other man hesitated. Fisk waved his gun around. "Stop delaying, Ben. Hand me the bag."

Sam didn't like the looks of the situation. He really didn't care if one of the crooks killed the other. He had planned, however, on bringing in both men as prisoners, simply as a matter of honor. It looked as if he would have to step in and take care of matters.

The sun had now risen above the hills. When he moved, he would have to move fast. Sam held his gun loosely, ready to use it if needed.

"You've been drinking," Ben said. "Maybe you should sober up a little. Don't want anybody to get hurt. Don't want to make a mistake, or something."

Fisk shot once. The bullet dug into the ground near Ben, kicking up dirt onto the other man's boots.

"Won't be no mistake. I want the money."

"Yes. I can see that now."

"It was just plain bad luck that the gold shipment wasn't there like it was supposed to be. That would have been plenty for everybody. But the way it turned out, there's barely enough for one. I plan to be the one. So just hand the bag over to me and we'll have no problems."

"Sure, Fisk. Whatever you say."

Ben slowly walked toward Fisk, holding the bag of bank loot in front of him.

Matt rode quickly toward the spot where he thought he had seen the flicker of a fire. It was still dark, but he could see well enough. The spot where the fire had been was closer than he realized, and he arrived at it sooner than he expected.

His arrival was also unexpected by the outlaw.

Tom had not yet gotten back on his horse

when Matt galloped toward him. He was so surprised that he did not even have a chance to pull his gun. Matt jumped from his horse's back without slowing. He landed on Tom, bringing him down.

Tom was still kneeling on the ground when he yelled, "Who in blazes are you?"

"Matthew Bodine, Texas Ranger," Matt answered. "You're under arrest!"

"Like hell I am!"

Tom had spent too much time in jail for his crimes. He didn't know what sentence a bank robbery would bring and he wasn't about to find out. He would do just about anything to keep from going back to jail. He ran toward Matt, hitting him solidly in the stomach with his shoulder. The outlaw was a big man and more solidly built than Matt expected. The blow had more force than expected. It knocked the wind out of him, forcing him to the ground. Tom made use of the advantage by kicking several times.

Though Matt took the blows, he was also figuring the strengths and weaknesses of his opponent. The outlaw was fighting hard, but it was more desperation than skill. Matt would therefore find his opening soon enough.

Matt rolled out of the way, tangling up the outlaw's legs in the process. Tom went down. Angrily, Matt also kicked, landing a solid blow to the other man's chin, snapping it back. It dazed the outlaw, though he came up swinging. Matt easily dodged the blows, moved in beneath them, and delivered a solid right to the chin.

The outlaw staggered back, but he remained conscious.

"I can bring you in easy, or I can bring you in the hard way," Matt said. "The choice is up to you."

"I heard there wasn't any law to worry about in this part of Texas," Tom wheezed, trying to catch his breath.

"Guess you heard wrong," Matt answered.

"Damn the luck . . ." Tom didn't finish the sentence. Instead, his hand reached for the gun on his hip. His hand didn't even touch the handle before Matt's gun blazed twice. The first bullet went through the fleshy part of Tom's gun hand. The second went through his shoulder. His arm was suddenly useless as the red seeped into his shirt from the wounds.

Dazed, he fell to his knees.

Matt approached the outlaw carefully, removed the gun from his holster.

"What's your name?" he asked.

"Tom Bunge."

"Tom Bunge, you're under arrest. I don't have any handcuffs, but I doubt if you'll give me any trouble. Not with that arm the way it is. Let me look at it. I think we can patch it up enough to stop the bleeding and get you to town."

"Ranger, who are you?"

"The name's Matthew Bodine."

Tom's eyes opened wider. "Matt Bodine—the gunfighter?" He gulped. "Damn. I could have been killed. I've heard about you. You could have killed me easy. Why didn't you kill me?"

Matt tore away the shirt, saw the wounds were clean, as he intended. They wouldn't be fatal.

"Didn't want to. I saw no need to kill you. And I want you to take me to your other two friends. I have a feeling this isn't the meeting place."

"Why would I do that?"

"It might help in your trial. It might keep me from killing you after all. You come up with your own reasons."

"Damn," Tom said. "You could have killed me. But you didn't. Guess I owe you something."

Matt picked up the bag.

"Is this all the loot?" he asked.

"The gold. The rest is there." He gestured at the small fire. "I got kind of angry at all that worthless paper. It wasn't all burned up. I suppose it might still be worth something."

"Pick it up. We'll bring it back. I don't want anybody to say that this Ranger left behind any of the evidence. Or the stolen money."

Tom's face was turning white as the shock wore off and he started to feel the pain of his wounds. He picked up the charred paper with his good hand.

"This was a lousy idea to start with," Tom muttered. "I should have gone on to Mexico years ago. Now, I guess it's too late."

"That's where you were heading? To Mexico?"

Tom shrugged.

"How about the others? What are their plans?"

"How am I to know? I barely knew them when we came up with this stupid plan."

"Where are you going to meet?"

"Down on the river. We're not that far away."

"Take me to the others."

"Guess at this point I don't have anything left to lose. Yeah. I'll take you to them."

Sam watched quietly as Ben neared Fisk with the bag of stolen money. Fisk unsteadily held the gun on Ben. Suddenly Ben swung the bag filled with gold and paper money. The blow was awkward, but hit Fisk in the face. His gun went off just inches from Ben's ear. The explosion almost deafened him, but he didn't back off. He swung the bag again, hitting a bruising blow to Fisk's shoulder. Ben dropped the bag and grabbed for the gun.

Sam decided he had waited long enough. He jumped up, raced toward the two, and shouted, "This is Sam Two-Wolves, Texas Ranger. You're both under arrest!"

The sound of his name and the title of Texas Ranger used in the same sentence almost made Sam smile, but his thought was cut short as bullets suddenly started flying in his direction. Fisk had managed to keep possession of the gun, and was now firing at Sam.

Sam fell to the ground and returned fire. From over a nearby hill, the sound of another, familiar gun was heard. Matt suddenly appeared, shooting fast and furious. His prisoner rode behind him, hands tied to the saddle horn.

Ben pulled his gun, but seemed unsure who to shoot at. Fisk took another shot toward Sam, then fired a shot at Matt. Sam took careful aim and shot once. His bullet hit the gun in Fisk's hand, shattering it and sending a bone-chilling pain through the outlaw's hand. The other outlaw quickly placed his gun on the ground and raised his hands in surrender.

Sam moved in to make the arrests.

"Just like you to make a big entrance," Sam commented dryly. "As it turns out, you really weren't needed. I have my two prisoners to your one."

"Don't underestimate my part in this arrest," Matt responded. "If not for me, you might have had a major fight on your hands."

"Well, maybe we both can claim credit . . ."

Matt interrupted his blood brother by raising his hand and pointing to another low hill to their left. "Was there a fourth outlaw in this gang?" he asked.

"Don't think so."

"Then who's the horseman riding this way—"

"As if we didn't know."

Josiah Finch came into view just as the sun shined brightly over the hills. He stopped his horse dramatically, kicking up dirt in front of Matt, Sam, and the outlaws they had just arrested.

"Looks like you all did a good job," he drawled.

"Aren't you maybe a little late?" Matt asked.

"Naw. I haven't had breakfast yet. So I figure the timing is just about right!"

Nine

Dingo Whaley was a straightforward man who involved himself in jobs that didn't require subtle planning: buffalo hunts, stagecoach robberies, bank holdups, killings-for-hire. He figured the same direct approach would work just as well south of the border.

Whaley was sitting at a table in a local cantina, just south of the border. Pierce and Jessup sat on either side of him. All three were drinking warm Mexican beer, though an unopened bottle of tequila sat in the center of the table. Empty chairs were across from the Americans.

"Where is this Raul Delgado character," Whaley asked.

"He'll be here," Jessup answered.

"My time is valuable," Whaley continued. "And Delgado is late."

His voice was calm, though anger was smoldering in his eyes. Jessup didn't like that look since he was the one that had arranged the meeting. If it didn't go right, Whaley's anger could be directed at him. When Dingo Whaley got mad, anybody around him could be a target.

"We're in Mexico now," Jessup explained. "They've got a different way of doing things down here. Besides, Delgado thinks he's some kind of bigshot. He's in charge of the federal forces in this part of the country, so I guess maybe he is. Maybe he's trying to play a game . . . wait you out."

"I don't like being made to wait."

"Give him ten more minutes?"

Whaley moved his glass across the table. His fingers were tense.

"Five minutes."

"Sure. That's plenty of time. While we're waiting, I'll order us another round."

Jessup motioned to the bartender and spoke in Spanish. "Over here! Another round! Pronto!"

The bartender was a large, surly looking man who was talking to several others at the bar. He glanced over at the table, then continued his talk as if he hadn't heard a thing.

Three minutes passed. Whaley looked at

him. Jessup called out again to the bartender. The bartender ignored him again.

Four minutes passed. Whaley pushed back his chair.

After four and a half minutes passed, a tall Mexican in a uniform stepped through the door. Some of the customers in the bar slipped out before the soldiers could block the doors. The ones that didn't make it moved quietly back to their tables. Delgado ignored everybody else and moved straight for the table. He sat down, pulled the cork from the tequila bottle with his teeth, and poured himself a glass. He drank it all down and poured another.

"You're not cutting that with anything?" Whaley asked in English.

"Do I look like some kind of pantywaist?" Delgado answered, also in English.

"I'm impressed. You know who I am. I know who you are. I want to do some business."

"You Americans are so direct," Delgado said. "I want to have another drink. From my personal stock." He raised a finger. The bartender jumped up, grabbed a bottle, and almost ran to the table.

Before the bartender made it even half way across the floor, Whaley exploded in a fit of rage. He pushed his chair back so hard that it fell over. He grabbed the bartender by the throat and started to shake him.

"You ignored us!" Whaley yelled, inches from the bartender's red face. "I don't like being ignored!"

Jessup nervously watched for Delgado's reaction. This was his territory, after all, and might not appreciate somebody else beating up on one of his citizens. He looked at his fingernails as Whaley yelled.

The bartender's face was getting redder by the second. Whaley slapped him once on both sides of the face. The sounds popped throughout the cantina. Everybody was now quiet, watching the American beat on the bartender. Whaley lifted him from the ground, punched him solidly in the gut. A groan escaped from the Mexican's lips. Whaley punched him again, then threw him to the floor. The tequila bottle slipped from his grasp and rolled several feet across the floor.

Whaley then really went berserk. He started to kick the bartender repeatedly. Bones crunched and blood streamed down the Mexican's face.

Finally, his anger spent, Whaley reached down, picked up the tequila bottle and placed it on the table. He was breathing slightly heavier than normal as he sat back down at the table.

"I hate being ignored," he explained to Delgado.

"I can see that. Quite a display, Señor Whaley. Is that how you treat everybody? Or just bartenders?"

"I'm generally quite reasonable," Whaley replied. "Ask my men here. Pierce? Jessup?"

"A picture of reason," Jessup said.

"Yep, always," Pierce said.

Delgado smiled.

"And your men are loyal to you?"

"Count on it. They know what's good for them."

The bartender was trying to crawl away. Delgado poured tequila from his bottle and motioned to two of his soldiers. "Help remove Carlos. And warn him next time to be more prompt in his service!" He laughed.

"Can we discuss business now?" Whaley asked.

"I admire your style," Delgado said. "I can see it gets results. Let's discuss what you have in mind."

Sam and Josiah Finch rode at front, followed by the three captured outlaws. Matt came up the rear.

"You boys were pretty slick, capturing these hooligans," Finch said. He was speaking softly. Sam had to ride fairly close to hear.

"Are these one of the gangs you've been after?"

"Unfortunately . . . no. These are some small-time hoods. I'm not complaining, mind you, especially since we got most of the money back. But these are just little fish, when it's the bigger fish I'm after. It's that Whaley gang that's really been giving me fits."

"You think Murdock is part of the gang?"

"Seems to me that it's a sure thing. I had a little chat with him last night before I rode out to find you and Matt. He didn't say much, but the way he said it confirmed to me that he's in with Whaley. I think there might be a way we can use that to our advantage."

"How is that?"

"We could track down the gang. I'm sure of it. But that would take time. We need to flush them out. Bring them to us. That gold shipment might be enough to entice them up to San Angelo. Then again, it might not be. If we could somehow get them to thinking that Murdock has turned on them and is singing to us, it might bring them up faster—to silence their boy. That combined with the gold would almost certainly lure them up here. Of course, we'd be ready for them."

110

"How would we get word to them? And make them believe it?"

"Sam, you're one of the best men I know, but you still have lots to learn. The criminal world has its own network. Word travels fast among the outlaws. We'll just help the rumors get started."

He nodded toward the three prisoners riding behind them. "We'll drop comments here and there, let them 'overhear' the talk. When we get to town, I'll have Leeds make sure that these prisoners are housed away from Murdock so they can assume the worst. We'll pick out one of the men and try to make a 'deal' with him, as well. It can be done."

"I'll let Matt in on the plan."

"Better yet, just start the talk with him. We're almost back to town. There'll be time. Remember, we can't be too obvious," Finch warned. "When we have an idea of where the gang has holed up, we'll let our fish swim away. Then we'll be waiting for them all with our net."

Delgado looked thoughtful as he twirled the tequila glass between his palms.

"What you are suggesting is quite illegal," he said. "Mexico has very strict laws, perhaps more strict than even the United States. We do not allow wrongdoers to go unpunished in our country. We search them out and issue swift and sure justice."

"No doubt of that," Whaley agreed. "I'm sure you run a tight ship. So, of course, I'll give you my word we would not violate any *Mexican* law. We are guests in your country. But if our . . . operations . . . all take place on the northern side of the Rio Grande, then we would not be violating your laws. And we would not insult you by offering a bribe. We would make appropriate gifts . . . and I will make sure that they are generous gifts."

Delgado sighed. "Our law does allow a certain tolerance in cases of pursuit. And Americans have little regard for international boundaries to start with. By law, we could not protect you."

"What if we could prove to you that your boundaries must be respected by American authorities?"

"Pardon me for being rude, but you do not look to be in the position to know your government's policy."

Whaley smiled, leaned back in the chair. "Jessup—show the *comandante* the papers."

Jessup took the papers stolen during the robbery out of his pocket, slid them across the table. Delgado snapped his fingers, and one of his men stepped forward, read them, and translated the words into Spanish.

This time it was Delgado's turn to smile.

"So, your government is investigating and is issuing orders that the boundary be respected. Invaluable information, Señor Whaley. That is information that I can use to further my . . . country's goals. I believe we can do business—up to a point. I will agree to overlook certain minor transgressions—unofficially, of course—that may occur during your excursions north. You may make whatever gifts you feel are appropriate. It will be to the benefit of Mexico."

Whaley held up his glass and toasted, "To Mexico!"

Delgado casually lifted his glass, took a drink, and continued, "Even though I admit your information is valuable, I do have access to a wider variety of sources than you. Perhaps I could share information with you as it becomes available."

"What kind of information?"

"For example, a gold shipment coming into Fort Concho in a matter of days. It is payroll for the soldiers stationed there. It is gold that could be used for good purpose in this country. For us to attack the United States would be an act of war. But if the gold were to be somehow rerouted . . ."

113

Whaley grinned. "I like your thinking. Very patriotic."

"I will check with my sources. I also have some plans involving your government friends from whom you stole those papers. I will get back with you. In the meantime, what is your next move?"

"Something simple. Maybe a stagecoach robbery. Just to keep sharp."

"How soon?"

"How about this morning?"

"Señor Whaley, you are truly a man of action. You are ruthless. And you are smart. But, then, so am I. It will make for an interesting partnership."

Sam had fallen back to ride beside Matt, behind the prisoners. They were near enough to San Angelo to see the outline of Fort Concho in the distance.

"Think these fellows will like the jail cells Finch picked out for them?" Sam asked, just loud enough for the three outlaws to hear. Ben was the one nearest him. He tried not to look interested as he listened.

"Not as much as Murdock likes his," Matt said. "Since he's cooperating in the case against the Whaley gang, he's doing well for himself."

"I don't understand some of these people," Matt said, shaking his head sadly. "How can anybody turn on their friends that way? Even to save themselves?"

"No honor among thieves," Sam suggested. "I'd be willing to bet, however, that Whaley would be quite interested in knowing about Murdock's working with the authorities."

"Yes, quite interested."

Colonel Leeds met the Rangers and their prisoners on the front step of his office. "You get rested up?" Finch asked.

"I feel quite well, thank you," Leeds answered. "I've already got my report prepared and filed."

"I bet you have!" Finch tossed down the bags of gold and paper and said, "Here's the money back. Here are the culprits. I'll take no credit for the arrests. It was all due to Matt and Sam."

"You two never cease to amaze me," Leeds said. "I'd rather have you two as friends than as enemies."

"We need a jail cell for these three," Finch continued. "Nothing as nice as you have for Murdock." He winked slightly. "I don't want any preferential treatment for these scoundrels."

"Whatever you say, Josiah. I'll see that they get what they deserve. I can find them a cell with all the creepy-crawly things imaginable and where they won't see daylight again."

Tom moaned at the thought of even more time spent behind bars. Fisk looked at the blood brothers and snarled with hatred. Ben fidgeted nervously with his tied hands but said nothing.

Finch dismounted as the prisoners were led away. "Now, for some breakfast . . ."

"Not so fast, Josiah." Leeds lowered his voice. "I wasn't the only one up bright and early. Those two government men—Easton and Holz—have been examining the records. They're inside, waiting for you. They want to talk."

"So we'll talk after breakfast!"

"They want to talk now. They seem to be aware of your reputation, and want to discuss a few items with you before you get away again."

Finch stood, arms crossed against his chest.

"You know how I feel about some empty-headed bureaucrats trying to tell me how to do my job!"

"Humor me, Josiah. All they want to do is to make a good appearance for their bosses in Washington. Let them do their dog and pony show and they'll be out of our hair in no time. I hope."

"Very well." He turned to Matt and Sam.

"Come on in, boys. We've had our fun. Now it's time to get to the really tough part of the job!"

Ten

Peter Easton was seated at Colonel Leeds's desk, papers spread in front of him. He had changed into the one suit that he had brought with him from the wrecked carriage. Carl Holz was seated at a small table across the room. He was working on a small notepad.

"Though I don't want to be here, might as well make the best of it," Easton said. "Sooner we get done, the sooner we can leave. Seems to me that we need to approach this problem on two fronts. One is talking with our men."

"Leeds seems cooperative enough," Holz suggested.

"So he does. He's a credit to the army. If he continues his good work, I'll be sure to recommend him for promotion. Then there are others . . ." He tapped the papers in front of him. "This Captain Josiah Finch of the Texas Rangers. Not only have complaints been filed against him, but he admits his deeds! He has never even tried to deny them!"

"I've asked around a little," Holz said. "The locals have great respect for him."

"But little respect for the southern border," Easton sniffed. "We will need to enlist his co-operation."

"He's out on a case now. Leeds has assured me that Finch will talk to us as soon as he returns."

"The second front is to appease our southern neighbors. Apparently Raul Delgado is the man in charge of the Mexican territory just south of here. We need to set up a meeting with him. Let him have his say. Make his complaints. Maybe it will quiet him down."

"I'll get the telegram out immediately, along with the one to D.C."

"Yes, by all means let them know we're on the job. See if you can arrange to have them send us some operating funds in that next gold shipment. While you're at it, see if you can arrange for some additional clothing. I'm afraid these could get stale quite fast. We can't have representatives of our federal government smelling like goats!"

Holz jotted a few more lines on his pad, then stood and walked over to the desk.

"Nothing wrong with your plan of action, Peter, but I have a question: How serious are we about this?"

Easton laughed politely. "Yes, I know what you're saying. I was sent to this forsaken land because I sniffed around in the wrong place. I doubt if anybody seriously expects us to solve the problem."

"Which is perhaps all the more reason to try and solve it," Holz suggested. "We've accomplished nothing so far but to lose our funds and our clothes. If we don't do *something* positive, we'll be the butt of jokes when we return home. We can kiss any further advancement good-bye."

"Unfortunately, you are right." Easton sighed again. "It's a confounded nuisance, but we will need to be firm. That means Leeds may have to enforce orders not to his liking." He scratched his head. "Can we issue orders to the army?"

"The army answers to the Department. We represent the Department. I'd say, yes, he'd have to do as we ask, whether he likes it or not."

"How about the Rangers?"

"They are under state jurisdiction. But I imagine they'll do as the army asks."

"And what might the army ask of the Rangers?" The voice was gruff and came from a small man just inside the doorway. He was carrying a big gun on his hip and his eyes shot fire. Beside him were Leeds and Matt Bodine and Sam Two-Wolves, the men that had rescued them the day before.

"We are interested in keeping international peace. We may look to the army to help enforce national and international law. What form that may take remains to be developed. That would obviously take precedence over state law . . . or personal preference."

"Hogwash," Finch said.

Leeds stepped forward. "Gentleman, this is Captain Josiah Finch of the Texas Rangers," Leeds said. "Josiah, this is Peter Easton and his assistant, Carl Holz."

"Bureaucrats," Finch spit out.

"Public servants," Easton said.

"Meddlers."

"So much for getting off on the right foot!" Sam said.

"Josiah always was one for diplomacy," Matt agreed.

Easton stood and walked around the desk. He stretched out his hand and said agreeably, "Let's not fight until we hear each other out. We are on the same side, after all."

Finch looked at the hand for long seconds, but finally stretched out his own hand. Easton then went around the room, shaking hands as if he were a politician running for office. "There! That's better. How does everybody feel about breakfast? Let's have a bite and then discuss business. Carl has some telegrams to send, then he will join us."

"You may not like what I have to say," Finch said.

"And you may not like what we have to say. But we are all reasonable men. We can work out the differences."

True to his word, Leeds put Tom, Ben, and Fisk in quarters that were worse than the cell occupied by Mel Murdock. The three outlaws were imprisoned in the building that had been the temporary jail while the permanent cells were being built. It was tiny, cramped, and dirty.

"I never should have gotten involved with you clowns," Fisk hissed. "I would have been better off had I just walked away."

"You were the one that talked us into the scheme," Ben said. "Our mistake was trusting you. You sure showed your true colors—of a skunk!"

Fisk leaped off his bunk and rushed toward Ben. Tom stood between them and separated them with his one good arm.

"We've all messed up," he said. "I've been

in too many jails in my time. I hate it here more than you two could possibly imagine. Instead of fighting each other, let's figure a way to get out."

Fisk spit and sat back down on his bunk.

"Get out? Sure. And then what? Those Rangers would be on our asses before we could even clear the city limits. What a brilliant idea."

"I overhead them talking," Ben said. "They've got Mel Murdock, one of the Dingo Whaley gang, in custody. They've got him in a nice setup, while we're here in this flea-infested dump. And you know why? Because they want Whaley and Murdock's cooperating with them. That's why."

"What's that got to do with us?" Tom asked.

"It could have a lot to do with us, if we could get out of here," Ben explained. "We've all heard of Dingo Whaley. He's a mean SOB, sure, but he knows how to get the jobs done. If we could hook up with him, we wouldn't have to worry about no second-rate heists. We'd be going first class."

"Right" Tom said. "He'd look at the great way we handled this robbery and take us in right away."

"He would if we had something to trade. We let him know about Murdock. That would help him. Then he might help us."

"You're crazy," Fisk said. "We'll never get out of here. And even if we do, Dingo Whaley wouldn't look at either of you twice."

"So what would you do if you could get out of here?"

"I'd kill that son of a bitch Sam Two-Wolves. My damned arm is still numb from where he shot the gun from my hand."

"Now who's dreaming?" Tom taunted. "You wouldn't last ten seconds in a fight with him. He's a regular gunslinger. Just like his partner, Bodine. Look at what he did to me. He could have killed me easily. You wouldn't have a chance."

"It was a lucky shot that got me," Fisk insisted.

"And you'll be six feet under while we're enjoying the good life with Whaley's gang!" Tom said, growing excited at the idea.

"Hell, even if you got out, you wouldn't know where to find that bunch. If the Rangers can't catch up to them, what makes you think you could?"

"We'd find them," Tom said stubbornly.

"Just leave me alone." Fisk leaned back on the bunk. "I need a drink."

Dingo Whaley sat on his horse at the side of the road, hidden by some brush. His men were positioned up and down the road. They were waiting for the stagecoach to pass. This was not one of the more popular routes, but it would have some mail and a few passengers, would give his men some more spending money, and it would be easier than hunting buffalo.

Whaley had to smile. The meeting with the Mexican official had gone better than he had hoped. Not only had Delgado agreed to not interfere with Whaley's operations, he would also provide information to help plan some big jobs! The idea of going after the gold shipment made his mouth water. Even without Delgado's share, it would make Whaley and his men rich.

The outlaw leader's thoughts were interrupted by the sound of a rushing stagecoach coming down the road. He saw the dust before he saw the horses and coach.

"Here it comes, boys!" he said. "Get ready!"

The outlaws put on their masks.

The stagecoach rounded the bend. Pierce, situated to get a good view of the road, took careful aim and followed the bouncing driver. He shot once. His big gun boomed and the driver slumped over, lifeless. The shotgun rider tried to determine where the shot had been fired from. Pierce's gun boomed a second time and the guard fell to the ground, rolled several times, and finally lay motion-less.

Two of Whaley's men rode into view, masks covering their faces, and grabbed the horses. A third man jumped into the driver's seat, took hold of the reins, and brought the coach to a stop.

Whaley and the others then galloped into the open. One man threw down the trunk containing the mail and broke it open. Jessup opened the door and ordered the passengers out. This time there were only a man and a woman. The man was dressed in an eastern suit. He reached into his belt and tried to pull a small gun. The outlaws opened fire, the guns exploded almost as one, and the man fell to the ground. Blood spurted from a dozen wounds, staining the dry ground.

The woman screamed and ran at Whaley. He laughed at first, then grew angry as her fingernails cut a gash in his cheek. He slapped her to the ground, almost knocking her unconscious. He pulled her to the side of the road, behind some brush, and pulled down his mask.

When he was through, even the other out-laws didn't want anything further to do with her.

Minutes later, the outlaws were back on

their horses and on their way back to Mexico, confident there were no witnesses.

The shotgun rider, however, had not been killed. The bullet had grazed him as the rocking coach tossed him from his seat. He landed hard, was knocked unconscious. He woke in time to see the group, led by Dingo Whaley, ride south toward the Mexican border. He recognized Whaley from seeing him around various saloons along the stage line. He watched for long minutes, to make sure they would not circle around. He decided that they were in fact headed for Mexico.

The guard painfully sat up, rubbed his bloody head. He already felt the throbbing. It would get worse before he got better, but at least he was alive.

He hobbled slowly along the road and found the dead male passenger. He had so many bullet holes that his body was already drained of blood. He looked a little further and found the female passenger, her body beaten beyond recognition. He climbed up to the seat, and found the driver slumped over, his chest blown open by a large-caliber gun.

He worked as quickly as he could, handicapped by the pain in his head and the hot sun, pulling the bodies to the side of the road. Burial would have to come later. Now, it was important to get word to the authorities about this latest robbery.

He climbed back up to the driver's seat, took reins in hand, and raced down the road. It would be miles before the next telegraph.

It didn't surprise Matt and Sam that Leeds suggested Rosie's place for breakfast. It was a good meal of bacon, eggs, hotcakes, and lots of coffee. Matt and Sam each ate three helpings, and complimented the cook.

Mary was again the waitress, providing special attention to Sam.

As Matt and Sam pushed back their plates, Finch asked, "Now, Easton, what is it you have to say to me? You bought breakfast, so I'll give you the courtesy of listening."

"As we were talking earlier, it's a question of boundaries. We have gotten lots of complaints about illegal excursions into Mexico. And, Captain Finch, your name has been associated with many of those incidents."

"That so?"

"It's all in the reports."

"Also in the reports are details about how Finch and his Rangers have brought many desperadoes to justice and brought at least a temporary peace to many of the rural settlements," Leeds said. "I know, because I wrote the reports."

Finch grinned. Easton continued, "Nobody doubts the achievements of the captain and his men. I saw first-hand their courage and skill when Matt and Sam came to our aid yesterday."

"And we weren't even Rangers, then!" Matt said.

Sam kicked him under the table. Matt gave him a dirty look. Easton seemed not to notice. He continued, "The question is a matter of how we keep peace with our Southern neighbor."

"Let me tell you something, *Mister* Easton," Finch said. "You bozos in Washington can make all the rules you want, but out there in the sagebrush those rules don't apply. Boundaries aren't lines on the ground, and nobody really knows where one country starts and the other stops. And then there are the corrupt officials who don't care who hides out down there. In fact, some of them encourage it, enjoying the damage the outlaws and bandits do to the Americans. When a lawbreaker heads south, I'm going after him, come hell or high water. You get it?"

Easton cleared his throat. "I'm sorry, Captain, but that can no longer be allowed. You are hereby ordered to remain on the United States side of the river."

Finch stood. "I'd like to see you try and stop me! I'll run over any man that tries and stop me!"

Holz hurried into the cantina, several slips of paper in his hand.

"Sorry I'm late, but . . ." He looked at the table, felt the tenseness in the air. "I see you all have already started discussing the business at hand." He waved the papers at Easton. "I have some telegrams here that might be pertinent."

"Let's hear them," Easton said.

Holz looked at the first one. "Raul Delgado is not only interested in meeting with us, he and a delegation will be arriving tomorrow to discuss the situation."

"Fast work," Leeds said. "That rascal has never been interested in talking with us before."

Holz looked at the second telegram. "The Department has approved a reduced amount for expenses . . . well, that's not of immediate interest to the army or Rangers, is it?"

"What about the third message?" Easton asked. Holz hesitated, tapped the paper against his leg. "Well, let's hear it!"

"It's news of a stage robbery. Apparently the Dingo Whaley gang is at work again."

130

Matt was nearest the federal representative. He reached out and plucked the paper from his hand and read it through.

"Apparently the gang killed two passengers—a man and a woman. And damned if they didn't head for Mexico!"

Eleven

The table was quiet for several minutes as the men thought about the latest news concerning the Whaley gang. Finally, Finch said, "Now you know why I've been after them. They've had quite a fling all across Texas, but now they're getting even bolder. It's more important than ever to stop them."

"So they were headed for Mexico?" Sam said. "Is that something new?"

"It is for the Whaley bunch," Finch answered. "Before, they split their time between legal or semilegal activities and their criminal activities. They moved across the state in no set pattern, which is one reason they've been difficult to locate. It seems that they've now decided to devote full-time to crime . . . and to set up a base of operations down south."

"We should be able to find them easier," Sam said.

"Except that it is in Mexico," Holz interrupted. "You can legally arrest them only on this side of the border, unless you go through the necessary paperwork as required by the Mexican government."

"Don't you ever get tired of talking?" Matt asked. "Sam and I could take care of this situation real easy. We could just go down there and bring him back—feet first, if necessary."

"There is no doubt that you, or any of the Rangers, could . . . 'take care of the situation,'" Easton said smoothly. "But it is important to first go through all the proper channels."

"Important for your career?" Finch asked.

"Important for all of us," Easton continued. "If we can keep the foreign government happy, our superiors will be happy. If you can bring in the criminals without violating law in return, your records will also be that much more distinguished. As I said, solving this problem appropriately is important for all of us. My heart goes out to those poor souls killed by the Whaley gang, but it does not change the basic situation."

Finch shook his head in frustration. Matt and Sam understood his feelings. They also knew that when the time came, each of them would do what needed to be done, regardless of what anybody said.

Easton moved the telegrams in patterns on the table in front of him. He said, "The commander of the Mexican forces in the area just south of the border has agreed to meet with us, and that is a positive development. That shows they are willing to work with us."

"Not necessarily." Leeds picked up the telegram from Delgado, looked at it as he talked. "I'm quite familiar with Raul Delgado. Our paths have crossed several times. There's even been rumors that his men have operated on our side of the river a time or two, though we've never had enough evidence to file formal complaints."

"That has never come to our attention," Holz said.

Leeds looked at him with narrowed eyes. "That is all in my reports, as well," he said. "If somebody didn't do enough research before starting down here . . . well, that's not my problem. Check with Washington if you don't believe me."

"What are you trying to say?" Holz asked.

Leeds slapped the telegram back on the table. "What I'm saying is don't trust this man too far. I wouldn't put *anything* past him. If he's willing to talk, that means he's got some-

134

thing up his sleeve. Don't get your hopes up for much cooperation from him."

"I understand your concern, Colonel," Easton said. "And, Josiah, I also understand your feelings. But I must again ask all of you to not take any rash actions until we can meet with Delgado."

"And in the meantime, how many more people are the Whaley gang going to kill?" Finch asked.

"Don't forget, Carl and I were also victims," Easton continued. "We have a personal stake in seeing Whaley brought to justice. At the same time, we cannot lose sight of the bigger picture."

"We cannot lose sight of the fact that people are getting killed," Finch said.

"Perhaps through the meeting we can reach an understanding that will solve the problems for everybody," Holz said.

"Fat chance."

Easton stood, and touched Holz lightly on the shoulder. He said, "Please excuse us, gentlemen. We need to prepare for the meeting with Delgado."

"Yes," Finch said. "Get out of here before I lose my temper!"

Easton touched the brim of his narrow-brimmed hat. Holz followed him out of the saloon.

* * *

Delgado sat at his desk, the telegram from the American official in front of him along with the official papers that Whaley had given him earlier. Most of Delgado's reports were not in writing. He preferred it that way. Many of his operations were not entirely legal, and he liked to keep his plans to himself as much as possible. The fewer people that knew about what was going on, the better he could control them. It wasn't like the Americans, who wanted to document every little thing.

For a long time, Delgado had itched to get his hands on some American gold, though up to now he had not seen how that could be arranged. He had crossed the border as many times as the Americans had, though he complained louder and longer than the Americans had to draw attention away from himself. Minor transgressions, however, were much different than committing a major crime, such as robbing a major gold shipment. Even so, Delgado had spies planted everywhere across southern Texas, on both sides of the border. He routinely heard the rumors, reports, and hard information about stage schedules, shipping plans, civilian and military operations. He was continually making, changing, and abandoning plans as the situations changed.

All this was with the tacit approval of his superiors in Mexico City, where the political situation was so unstable that nobody paid much attention to a single commander in a rural outpost. As long as he didn't rock the boat, they left him alone.

Dingo Whaley approaching him was a stroke of luck. It was nothing new for outlaws to operate out of Mexico. Sometimes he let them work without interference, sometimes he cooperated with American authorities, depending on what he needed at any given time. That Whaley had the balls to actually try to ally himself with Delgado earned his respect. The Whaley gang also probably had the balls to actually carry off a gold theft, without casting any suspicion on Delgado!

The Mexican official reviewed in his mind the information he had been gathering about the gold shipment so that he could share it with Whaley. That was still several days away, which would give him time to meet with the Americans and to help Whaley draw up his plans.

And to make matters even better, the Americans wanted to set up a meeting with him to discuss the border crossing question! He would be more than willing to talk with them. For all the good it would do them. They would also be playing into his hands.

It couldn't be working out any better than if he had planned it that way to start with.

"Just calm down, Josiah," Colonel Leeds said. "I saw the way you wanted to thrash Holz. That wouldn't solve anything."

"I know. But it sure would be fun."

"What's important now is to find a way to get the Whaley gang without crossing the border, if we can," Sam said.

"You are a fast learner, Sam," Finch said. "We started the plan on the trail, making Fisk and his bunch think that we let slip information that could be valuable to Whaley. Sam, I want you to talk with one of those yahoos, in private. Act like you're trying to make a deal with him . . . like we have presumably done with Murdock. That should clinch the idea in their minds. We also need to make sure they know that Whaley gang is down in Mexico, so that they'll be pointed in the right direction when they 'escape' from our custody. Once word gets out through the outlaw grapevine that they have information for Whaley, he will find them."

"With Sam's gift of gab, that should be easy," Matt said.

"No problem," Sam agreed.

"I can almost guarantee that Whaley will

try to kill Murdock for 'squealing' on him. That will bring him to us. I don't like having to wait for him to show up, but I think it's a safe bet that he will show."

"What do you want me to do?" Matt asked.

"I want one of us guarding Murdock when the time comes. There's also the question of the gold coming in, which I promised the colonel to help guard. You can help me work out those arrangements. I want to go over his town in detail. I want to arrange things so that during the escape, nobody gets hurt. I want to be ready for the planned attack on Murdock. I want to safeguard the gold."

"I appreciate the effort of you and the boys," Leeds said.

"It'll be our pleasure," Matt said.

Holz and Easton walked slowly back to the colonel's office. The sun was hot and sweat was already soaking their suits.

"I think we're fighting a losing battle," Easton said. "And, to be honest, I'm wondering if it's a fight we should lose."

"Are you serious, Peter? We can't fail. Especially you, since you're already in the doghouse . . ."

"I'm having second thoughts about this whole mission," Easton said. "These are all good men, doing their jobs the best way they know how. They're just trying to stop the robberies and killings. Maybe that's more important than a single man's career."

"Speak for yourself. Maybe your career isn't that important, but mine is. I've gambled everything on coming here with you. I don't intend to fail."

"And we won't fail. The meeting with Delgado might prove beneficial. Leeds, though reluctant, has agreed to help enforce the dictates against crossing the border. We'll just do the best we can, make our report and recommendations—that will probably be buried and forgotten in a matter of weeks, in any case—and get back home."

"I still have to question how serious you are about this mission," Holz said.

"Question all you want. I'm still in charge, and I'll call the shots. So for now I want you to start making arrangements for Delgado's visit. You know the routine. Make him feel like somebody important, since we want his cooperation. Arrange some kind of dinner or something."

"In *this* town?"

"Talk to Leeds. I imagine Rosie can come up with something. Leeds will have some kind of facility where we can have more formal surroundings. Stop griping and make it work."

The corporal on guard duty knocked on the door to the cramped cell.

"Hey, Tom, you got company!"

He scratched some bites that he had received during the night from the little creatures in his bunk. Though he had spent time in jail, he never got used to it.

"Yeah? Who is it? Unless they're to get me out of here, I'm not interested . . . and I don't think there's much chance of that."

"Maybe we should talk before you jump to conclusions," Sam said.

"I'm especially not interested in talking with *you*. Just leave me alone."

Sam motioned to the corporal, who opened the door and grabbed Tom by the arm, lifting him off the bunk.

"Easy, soldier," Sam said. "Can't you see the shoulder is bandaged?"

Tom shook off the hand and stood on his own. He walked in front of the corporal into an adjoining room. The old adobe building had been almost abandoned, and was used mainly for storage. An old desk was still in the room, piled high with trash. Sam pushed the trash off the desk and sat on a box. He left the door open a crack so that they could be overheard by the other two still in the cell.

"Have a seat," Sam said, pointing to the only chair in the room. "Let's chat for a little while."

"We have nothing to talk about. I messed up again. I did the crime. With my record, I know they'll send me to the pen again. You can't threaten me with anything that I don't already know about."

Sam leaned back in his chair, put his feet on the desk. "I'm not here to threaten you. What I have to say might help you."

"You're a lawman. I haven't seen a lawman yet that's willing to help me."

"I'm offering you a chance to work with us. If you cooperate, it'll go easier on you. Take a look at Murdock. He's cooperating with us, and look how it's working out for him. He's not in a cramped cell with two other men. Do you think he's getting the same kind of slop to eat as you are? Do you think he'll be hanged, as he should be?"

"So he squealed on his gang. Whaley won't stand for it. He'll be dead, even if he doesn't hang."

Sam shrugged. "The Whaley gang is now in Mexico. They have no idea that Murdock is cooperating, and there's no way they could know. They won't know until it's too late. Murdock doesn't have anything to fear. And we will get Whaley eventually. At that time,

Whaley will be behind bars or hanged, while Murdock will probably be done with whatever time he has to serve. You could get the same deal. You didn't plan the bank robbery. Just be willing to testify against Fisk and we'll make it easier on you."

"I've done lots of things wrong in my life, but I've never squealed," Tom said.

"Think about it. You may never get another chance."

The corporal led Tom back to his cell, slammed the door behind him. Fisk noted that as the door slammed, dust rose in puffs from the bars on the window. The soldier went back to the adjoining room, leaving the prisoners to themselves.

"He wanted me to squeal on you," Tom said. "I wasn't interested."

"The SOB," Fisk said. "The fool left the door open and we heard it all. I'm going to kill that Two-Wolves. It's not bad enough that he shoots me, he's trying to place all the guilt on me. Good thing you didn't cooperate, else I'd have to kill you, too."

"Give it a rest," Ben said. "Two-Wolves said lots more that's even more interesting. Did you hear that talk about Murdock, and how he's turned on Whaley? Like we were talking earlier, that is something that we could use . . . if we could get out of here and get word to Whaley." He sat down on his own bunk. "I guess that's just so much crap. We'll never get out of here."

Fisk paced back and forth, pounding his fist on the wall. Each time his fist hit, another cloud of dust spurted out of the old adobe wall.

"Wait a minute," he said, beating the wall around the window. "Maybe there is a way, after all. This old building is about to fall apart. Maybe with a little luck, and a little work, we could get out of here." He poked around the bars on the windows. "Take a look at this. With some luck, maybe we'll be out of here, after all."

"Then we can be on our way to Mexico," Tom said. "If we can get in good with Whaley, we'll have it made!"

"We'll head for Mexico," Fisk said. "After I kill Sam Two-Wolves."

Twelve

Sam unexpectedly had some time to kill. He would eventually find Josiah and Matt and help them in their planning, but for now he decided to enjoy the sunshine, which was common in this part of Texas. Though Sam was a Cherokee, with an Indian's appreciation of nature, he had attended school in the East, where he had gained an appreciation for art and architecture.

He walked along the street. Leeds had told Sam that Fort Concho was built of limestone by German craftsmen. Sam admired the buildings, which contrasted with the adobe structures that existed in most of the town. The fort also looked rather stately compared to the wrecked look of the rest of San Angelo, which was periodically on the receiving end of ravages by buffalo hunters and other rough characters.

Sam wondered if Fisk and the others would take the bait about Murdock. Wouldn't they be suspicious that Sam had revealed so much about Whaley's gang, especially when they found that the old adobe had started to deteriorate around the bars in the window, making escape possible? Sam would not have fallen for the trick, but Josiah figured they would, and he was a good judge of men and the criminal mind. In any case, Sam had done his job. The trap was baited. Matt and Josiah would set it. Then it would be a matter of patience, to see if the prey would fall for the trap.

Sam approached Rosie's cantina. Curious, he looked inside, but Mary was not there. Though the others kidded him about Mary's interest in him, Sam really thought she was a sweet girl. He didn't like to wear his heart on his sleeve, and preferred that not even Matt know too much about his romantic interests, though there was no malice involved. Sam had to admit that he was just a little disappointed that Mary was not there, since he would have liked to talk with her a little, away from the crowd.

He turned around, to walk toward the colonel's office, when a familiar figure raced around the corner and ran into him. Mary's face at first was flustered, as a basket of fruit

146

in her arms bounced into the air. Sam caught it before any of its contents could hit the ground. Mary's face brightened with a grin when she recognized Sam as the man standing above her.

"Sam! I'm sorry to run into you . . . I should have watched where I was going . . ."

"My pleasure, Mary." He held the basket in one hand, reached out to her with the other. "May I help you up?"

Mary had long, dark hair and smooth skin that contrasted with the low-cut white blouse she was wearing. Her long, colorful skirt was tangled around her ankles. She reached up to Sam, who enjoyed the view that his angle provided. Her hand lingered on his a little longer than might have been expected. She smiled as she unselfconsciously rearranged her blouse and skirt.

"Thank you, Sam."

"I was hoping to see you. I looked in at Rosie's, but you weren't there."

"Really?" She tossed her head. "I couldn't have told it by the cool way you've been treating me at Rosie's. I figured I just wasn't good enough for you."

"Guess I'm just naturally shy. Not like Matt."

"I can't imagine either of you being shy . . . about anything. The way you came to our aid at the cantina when those hooligans tried to mess with us . . . you were wonderful!"

Sam laughed. "Sometimes we're more bold than others. Depends on what we're up against. Now, a pretty woman like yourself . . ."

"Yes?"

Sam decided to change the subject.

"Why the hurry? And what's with the basket of fruit? Rosie's seems more like a frijoles-and-tortilla place."

"It's for the dinner. Surely you know about it? There's an important official from Mexico going to meet with Colonel Leeds and those two federal officials."

"Important official? You must mean Delgado. I'd probably call him a two-bit crook . . . but I'm not a diplomat."

"Yes. Raul Delgado. Colonel Leeds will conduct a dinner for him. Rosie will take care of the arrangements and I am helping Rosie. The colonel has a dining room he uses for such occasions. That is where I am headed now. Would you join me?"

"If I could have a favor."

Mary smiled and said, "Name it."

"Allow me to assist you with your load."

The two walked in the sunshine. Sam carried the basket easily in his left arm. His right hand kept trying to put itself around Mary's slim shoulder, and she did not push it away.

"No, Sam, you are not shy," she said. "Not shy at all!"

"Do you object?"

"Of course not! I meet lots of men in my job at Rosie's, but few of them hold any interest for me. They tend to be loud and crude cowboys, soldiers, buffalo hunters. Some of them are quite wealthy. Some are handsome. A few are even nice. But I don't want to go away with them, not even for a night."

"So why'd you single me out?"

"There is something about you that is different . . . something that sets you apart from other men. You interested me. But I suppose to you I'm just another saloon girl."

Sam winced, remembering the words he had used when he first met Mary.

"I apologize for being so harsh," Sam said. "It was thoughtless of me."

Mary looked at him through half-closed eyes. "I'm not mad about it. What you said is true. I'm not much more than a barmaid, though I'd like to be more. I'd like to find a good man and live on a ranch. I'd like to have the family I never had. Rosie took me in when I was just a girl, gave me a place to live and a job to do. She was kind to me, good to me. But I would like to have a family of my own and a home of my own. Though I will not settle for a man I do not love."

149

"I definitely owe you an apology," Sam said. "Will you accept my apology?"

Mary nodded her head.

The walk went much too quickly.

"Here is the dining hall," Mary said. "Why not step inside and look at the arrangements?"

Sam was stunned when he stepped through the door. Tables were set up covered with spotless white cloths. The chairs were polished wood. Shiny glasses and silverware were on the table. It was as nice as many of the dinner parties he had attended while attending the eastern university.

Leeds and Rosie were talking between themselves in the far corner of the room.

"Sam!" Leeds called out. "Glad you're here. What do you think?"

"Amazing," Sam said, truthfully. "How can you manage all this?"

"Rosie's a magician. I'm allowed a certain amount of funding for entertainment, and in my business if you don't entertain visiting officers well, you might as well kiss off any chance for promotion. You learn some tricks. But this is all Rosie's doing."

Sam looked around again. "This is all quite impressive, but what's the hurry? You just got the telegram from Delgado this morning."

"Trust me, even starting now, Rosie will be busy up to the time of the dinner itself."

"Why go to all this trouble?"

"It's part of the job. But don't worry. You, Matt, and Josiah are all invited, as well."

Matt looked over a large safe in a room near the office of Colonel Leeds. The safe was built into a wall that was reinforced with iron and heavy wood, though it was designed to blend in with the rest of the fort. It was better constructed than the adobe-and-wood bank building down the street that had been reduced to rubble by the attempted bank robbery.

"The gold will go right in there," Finch said. "I suspect it'll take more than dumb luck to get into this safe. Especially considering that Sam will be here to guard it."

"And you will be watching Murdock," Matt said. "You being there by yourself makes me nervous. You need at least some backup . . ."

"No. I want the element of surprise. There'll be a few soldiers posted around town, but if we have too many men kicking around, it'll muddy the waters and Whaley's gang will pass us right by. Trust me. My plan will work."

"I still don't know. There's an awful lot of uncertainty about all this."

"Hell, boy, life is uncertain. Sometimes you

151

just take your chances. You know that better than me, some of the chances you take!"

"That's different. Those chances are when I can depend on myself, or on somebody I know I can depend on, like you and Sam. Those clowns in the old jail are a different matter. What if they don't figure out that the bars on the window are loose? Will we have to go in and help plan their escape for them? And what if they decide that it'd be better to stay clear of Whaley and his gang? Then where are we?"

"If that happens, we'll just come up with a different plan. But I have a feeling about those three. I think they'll take the bait. They're all small-time hoods, wanting a crack at the big time. They know they could never do it on their own. If they ever had any doubts about that, you and Sam put them at rest when you captured them so easily after the failed bank robbery. No, their only chance is to join up with somebody much bigger than they are . . . somebody like Dingo Whaley."

Finch stood on a chair to examine the only window in the room. It was a small opening that would let light in but would not provide easy access from the outside.

"And what if Whaley doesn't take the bait?"

"I've followed Dingo Whaley for a while

now. I can almost tell you how he thinks. He cannot let one of his men turn on him and live. It'd just not be like him. And then there is the gold shipment, coming in later in the week. I have a feeling he'd like to get his hands on that gold. When you mix together revenge on Murdock and greed for the gold . . . Whaley will be here. And he'll be here within the week. You can count on it."

"You seem very sure of yourself."

"When you work with outlaws as long as I have, you develop a sixth sense about these things."

"With any luck, I don't plan to be that intimate with outlaws for that long."

"You mean you don't plan to make the Texas Rangers your career?" Finch laughed. "No, you and Sam are too young, with too much mischief in you yet. But you never know what life has in store for you."

"How's the gold coming in? By special carrier?"

"No. It'll be on a regular stage, to keep from drawing attention to itself. But it will be more heavily guarded than usual. All the 'passengers' will be guards. And there'll be soldiers stationed along the route. These are rather unusual precautions, but probably smart, considering how many robberies there's been recently. An attempt might be made on the stage itself, but I think any try for the gold will come here, not on the road."

"You've figured all the angles, haven't you, Josiah?"

"That's what I'm paid to do."

Matt and Josiah were having lunch when a sudden disturbance outside caught their attention. Josiah looked outside and said, "A little excitement going on. Let's take a look."

Matt followed Finch into the street, where a Mexican official and a dozen soldiers were riding. They wore dress uniforms and shiny swords.

"That's Raul Delgado," Finch said.

"Am I supposed to be impressed?"

"He'd think you should be."

Delgado continued to the office normally used by Colonel Leeds. This time, two civilians came out to greet him.

"I am Delgado," the rider said. "Tell Colonel Leeds I am here for his meeting."

The portly man cleared his throat and said, "Excuse me, Commander. I am Peter Easton. This is my associate, Carl Holz. We are representatives of the United States government, and the ones who invited you to a meeting. You must have rode very quickly to make such good time."

"When important business is involved, time is of the essence."

Leeds hurried down the street.

"So, Commander Delgado, you decided to meet with us, after all?"

"Good afternoon to you, as well, Colonel Leeds. There are many important issues to discuss. The time seemed right for a meeting. So here I am."

Easton said, "Some quarters will be made available for you to freshen up for tonight's dinner. We've arranged something special for you, after which we can discuss business."

"I wouldn't miss this for the world."

Fisk continued to work on the crumbling adobe of the cell window. For the past two days, he had taken turns with the other two as they scraped and dug at the dirt, which originally had been hard as stone but now was soft and yielding to their efforts. They had had to stop their work several times as a guard wandered in to check on them. Most of the day, however, they had been left alone.

They were hindered by a lack of tools, but Ben helped solve that problem by removing his belt buckle. It was sharp enough to dig into the material and crumble it enough to get a fingerhold. The work was slow, but progress was being made.

It was now nearly dark as the guard brought the evening meal. Down the road, some music and noise could be heard coming from the fort.

"Now they're having some damned party," Fisk grumbled. "Hey, guard! What's going on at the fort?"

This time the guard was a private. He took the empty plates and answered, "Some official from down south. They're throwing some kind of powwow for him. Why, are you looking for an invitation or something?"

The guard laughed.

"Maybe we are, at that," Fisk said.

"I'm sure. All the big guys in town will be there. The colonel. His officers. The bank president. The mayor. The federal guys. Even the Texas Rangers. I'm sure you all would fit right in!"

"Hey, would you ask them to keep it down? We'll be trying to sleep in here tonight!"

The guard laughed and shook his head as he closed the door behind him.

"Are you crazy or something?" Tom asked.

"Naw. You saw how funny that guard thought the idea of us getting out was. They'll never expect us to really get out tonight. And if the soldiers are up at the party, there'll be fewer left to come after us."

Ben moved back to the window and started working again.

"I think we're just about deep enough," he said. "I thought I could feel the bars give a little. Come on over and help me."

The three men grabbed hold of the bar on the left and started to twist. Even with the old adobe, the bars were still fairly solid and refused to budge at first. With all three men straining, the first bar moved slightly. This gave them new energy. Ben dug into the adobe as Tom and Fisk continued to twist and strain at the bar, until finally the wall started to crack and the bottom of the bar came free with such force that it almost hit Tom in the face.

By now it was entirely dark. There was no sound from the adjoining room. The prisoners figured that the guard was probably sleeping, but still tried to work quietly.

The second bar came out a little easier, and the final ones easier still. The men placed them quietly on the floor.

"I'm out of here," Tom said, pushing himself into the opening. "I've had all I ever want of jail cells."

"We'll need to find some horses," Ben said. "If the soldiers are all at the party, we should

157

be able to find a few left unguarded. Maybe even a few guns. Then we're on our way to Mexico."

"You two do what you want," Fisk said. "But I have my personal business to attend to."

"You still think you can take out Sam Two-Wolves?" Ben said. "Go for it. He'll skin you alive. And I can't say it wouldn't happen to a nicer person. I only wish I could stick around to see it."

Tom added, "It's your business, and I could care less. If we hadn't listened to you in the first place, we wouldn't be here now. I'm going to find Whaley."

"You'll see. I'll take out Two-Wolves and still be in Mexico before you two. Then we'll see who has the last laugh."

Tom and Ben slipped into the night toward the stable, figuring there would be some horses there that they could steal.

Fisk moved toward the sounds of the party coming from the fort.

Thirteen

It took some doing, but Matt and Sam were able to find new suits at the only store in town and have a local seamstress fit them before the dinner party started. It took even more doing to convince Josiah Finch to accept a new suit as a gift and to actually wear it.

"Consider it another sacrifice for your state and your country," Sam suggested.

"Hell, I'd rather be out chasing Indians and outlaws," Finch responded.

"It's an honor to be invited to such a diplomatic dinner," Matt continued.

"I think I'd rather be at my own scalping," Finch said.

But the Texas Ranger put on the new suit and joined Matt, Sam, and Leeds at the function. Sam had an idea what to expect, since he had seen a preview. Matt, however, was taken completely by surprise when they walked in and saw the dazzling display.

"I can hardly believe this," he said. "Colonel, how were you able to manage this?"

"I give credit to Rosie," Leeds answered. He was dressed in his best uniform. "I don't know what I'd do without her. I'd put her up there with those Washington women any day of the week." He lowered his voice, and continued confidentially, "In fact, I'm planning just that. I'm going to ask her the question probably later tonight, after this is all over."

"Good luck," Finch said. "You have my blessing, or my sympathy, whichever is most appropriate."

"Thank you, Josiah."

He looked around the room, which was now starting to fill with people. He said, "I still don't understand why all the fuss. You're treating this guy like he's actually somebody important."

Leeds sighed. "You and I know what Delgado really is. I've had dealings with him and know the truth all too well. Unfortunately, he is also the ranking official in the territory that adjoins ours. And this is politics, whether we like it or not."

"Where is the SOB?"

"Diplomacy, Josiah," Sam said, smiling. "Remember? Diplomacy."

160

"Where is the distinguished and honorable SOB?"

"He'll make a late entrance, just to show how important he is. He should be here soon."

Barney Cooper, the bank president, and two others walked up to the group. He shook Matt's hand, then Sam's.

"This is Alex Granger and Dennis Johnson, two of the larger stockholders in the bank association," Cooper said. "We just wanted to personally thank you for your excellent work the other night. Thanks to you, virtually all the money was recovered. If not for you Rangers, they might have gotten completely away!"

"It was nothing," Sam said.

"Just doing our duty," Matt said.

"We are all safer with you men here," Cooper concluded. "Hope you all stay with it for a long time. We all need you."

As the group blended in with the growing crowd, Matt asked Finch, "How much did you pay him to tell us that?"

The Ranger captain laughed and said, "Didn't have to pay him a thing. Thanks like that are one of the fringe benefits of the job. The bad thing is that if you mess up, the same man would probably be in charge of the grievance committee looking to file a complaint against you. It's all part of the job."

161

"And in the end, the pay's the same?"

"Son, if you do this kind of work for the pay, you're just plain crazy. Of course, you're probably crazy if you do this kind of work for *any* reason."

Leeds spoke up then. "Excuse me, will you? There's the man of the hour. I need to go and do my job."

Delgado entered the room with Carl Holz and Peter Easton. They took the head table, and were joined by Leeds. Some of Delgado's men came up the rear. They remained standing. Leeds motioned to the Rangers to join them as well.

"Guess this is your lucky day, Josiah."

"You mean I got to eat with those yahoos, as well? I don't know how I let you boys talk me into this!"

"Consider it part of the job!"

Ben and Tom had no problem finding horses. The stable was deserted and the two had their pick of horses and gear. They didn't bother to be choosy, but grabbed the first saddles they found and tossed them on the backs of the first horses they came to. In minutes, they were out the back door and on their way to Mexico. They were pleased that nobody had seen them or tried to stop them. They hoped that by the time the jailbreak was discovered, they would be almost to Mexico.

Fisk was not in such a hurry, since he was more concerned about the party. He made a circle around the stable, watched his fellow ex-prisoners ride into the night toward the south. He had no plan except for his hatred of Sam Two-Wolves. He would find some way to get even for humiliating him and trying to pin all the blame for the botched bank job on him!

His path took him past Rosie's cantina, which was now locked and dark. Fisk stopped, looked through the window into the dark interior, and saw the bottles lined up behind the bar. He went around the back, kicked open the door. He waited for several seconds and entered when nobody confronted him. He grabbed the first bottle he found, took a long drink, felt the warmth go inside him. He found a smaller bottle, put it in his pocket, and started looking around.

Fisk located a gun and holster in the small area at the back of the cantina that Rosie used as an office. Fisk guessed that it had been used as payment by some out-of-work cowboy, or perhaps it was even left behind from the shoot-out that had taken place previously. It didn't really matter, since it was a weapon and it would be enough to take care of Sam Two-

Wolves. He checked the action, made sure the cartridges were good, and strapped the holster around his waist.

He suddenly felt a lot better. His doubts started to vanish. Now he had to find Two-Wolves, who would be at the party.

Fisk snatched another bottle as he left the cantina and worked his way toward the fort, keeping to the shadows. He fingered his gun, took another drink, until he reached a window and looked inside. The men inside were seated at fancy tables, eating fancy food, and Sam Two-Wolves was at the head table, as if he were somebody important. How important would he be with a bullet through his heart?

The outlaw pulled his gun, aimed through the window, but paused as first one official and then another stood to make speeches, blocking a clear shot at Two-Wolves. Fisk stayed back in the shadows, waiting for the right moment.

Leeds finished introducing everybody around the table as Mary and some of Rosie's other girls started to serve the food. They wore spotless, freshly pressed uniforms. Matt was amazed at the magic Rosie had cast over the meal, as well: fresh beef, fresh vegetables, cold wine. Delgado was charming as he ate, polite to everybody, including Finch and Leeds.

"He's slick," Leeds whispered at one point to Matt. "Don't let it fool you."

"It doesn't," Matt answered. "I can recognize bull, no matter how slick the package."

The evening continued. The mayor made a small speech. Easton made an introductory speech. Then it was Delgado's turn. He spoke in English to the group.

"It is with great pleasure that I greet my friends to the north," he said. "Our intent is to further beneficial relations between the countries, through mutual respect and cooperation. In that I seek your help . . . respect . . . and cooperation."

"He *is* good," Sam agreed as the crowd applauded.

Delgado bowed and returned to his seat.

As Rosie's girls started to serve the dessert, Leeds leaned over the table and said, "Those were good words, Delgado. Maybe it's time now to get down to business. Just what are you doing up here?"

Holz started to interrupt. "Colonel! Now is not the time. . . ."

Delgado raised his hand. "No. We can start our discussions now, if you wish. You know the problem. You Americans have no respect for the border. You treat my country as if it were your private lands. That must stop. And it must stop immediately."

"Delgado, we both know you violate the border as much or more than we do. The difference is that we go down to arrest those that have committed crimes in our country. Your people come up here to commit crimes."

"Colonel, those are harsh words." He turned to Easton. "Is this any way to treat a guest in your country? I thought we were here to solve problems."

"Leeds, that's enough," Easton said.

"The idea is to discuss all sides of the issue, not to whitewash it."

"We have been very patient," Delgado continued. "But since you gentlemen speak plainly, so will I. The problem has gotten to the point that if you Americans set foot on Mexican soil without permission, for any reason, we will arrest them. It is as simple as that."

Easton asked, "Can you be serious? We are here to solve the problem. You give us no room to negotiate."

Delgado looked straight at Josiah Finch. "We are not joking," Delgado said.

If the Ranger started to retort, the words never got out of his mouth, as a shot exploded through a window in the back of the dining

166

room. Glass showered the tables as the slug hit the wall behind Sam's head.

Somebody screamed as people dived under the tables. Delgado's men pulled their guns and were ready to return fire. He stopped them with a single command.

Sam knew the bullet must have been intended for him since he heard it whistle past his ear. He pulled his own gun and ran across the floor, leaping through the window in an attempt to confront the attacker. Parts of the glass remained in its frame and was shattered as Sam's body leaped through it.

He landed on his feet and started looking around carefully. Another shot blazed from behind a tree. There were still too many people around to get in a full-fledged gunfight, so Sam did not shoot back. Instead, he circled around so that if he drew fire it would be away from the building.

Who could be shooting at him? And why just him?

Another shot. Sam fell to the ground and the bullet passed harmlessly overhead.

"Damn . . . and a new suit, too!" he muttered.

Fisk knew the moment had come. The speeches had all been made and everybody was again seated at their tables, giving him a clear shot at Two-Wolves. He took careful aim, fired. And missed. He had missed by only inches . . . but it was still a miss.

Suddenly, everything was chaos inside the building and he looked up in time to see Two-Wolves running across the room toward him. Fisk quickly retreated. He didn't want to face the full fury that Sam could unleash.

Sam vaulted through the window, landing where Fisk had stood just moments before. Fisk ran, took another shot, and missed again.

Fisk was suddenly not so sure of himself. He realized now that he should have thought his plan through in more detail. He had failed to kill Sam. He had no horse on which to escape. He had no escape plan. With a panicky feeling, the thought hit him that he might not even make it out of this situation alive.

He should have joined the other two for Mexico. Now it was too late. He had no choice but to see this through to the end.

Sam had slipped into the shadows, looking in every bush and behind every tree for his attacker. In minutes, the others would be out here as well. Sam, however, did not want any help on this one. He took a dim view of people trying to kill him. He wanted to deal with his assailant on his own.

"Who are you?" he asked. "Why do you want to kill me?"

"Sam Two-Wolves," Fisk called out, his voice a little hoarse. "You've humiliated me. You've accused me. Now it's time for you to die."

"Fisk? So you managed to escape, have you? You would have been better off staying in your jail cell." Sam paused, moved to the next bush. "What about the other two? Are they out, too? Are they with you?"

"Why don't you go and find out for yourself? I don't keep track of them. That's your job."

Sam figured Fisk was working alone, since he had heard only the one voice and the one gun being fired. Perhaps the other two were on their way to Mexico, as Finch had predicted. That Fisk had stayed behind was a development that Finch had not predicted. But, then, nobody was perfect.

"You can't win, Fisk. In seconds, this place will have more men hunting for you than you could imagine. You'll be shot to ribbons. Give yourself up—again—and you might live."

"Not until I kill you first!"

Sam saw the glint of light on metal, hit the ground again as Fisk fired. Sam shot, but the bullet hit a tree.

"Tell you what, Fisk. I'll make it a little

fairer for you. Come out in the open and I'll holster my gun. I'll even let you draw first. Or you don't even have to draw, if you want. Just give me to the count of three." Several figures appeared from the building. Sam called out, "Nobody shoot! I'm giving this fellow a chance to fight me fair and square. He's thinking about it!"

"What is he, a coward?" somebody called out.

"Come on out and fight like a man!" another voice called out.

Fisk knew he was trapped. There was no chance for escape. He could be killed by the bullets of a dozen men, all out for blood. Or he could go out like a man, in a fair fight with Sam Two-Wolves.

"You've got a deal," he said. "I'm coming out. Then we'll see who's the better man."

Same slowly placed his revolver back in its holster and waited for Fisk to show himself. Fisk was strangely calm as he stepped into the open area illuminated by the light from inside the dining hall. He returned his gun to its holster and stood with his hand outstretched.

He realized that a crowd was now watching. It was perhaps the biggest crowd that had ever watched him do anything. If he was to die, at least he would not die a coward.

Sam stood comfortably in the shadows, waiting for the other man to make his move.

"You can still back out," Sam said.

"No. I still plan to kill you. Or I will die trying."

His hand dropped to the gun. He had it almost out of the holster when Sam's gun exploded. The slug hit Fisk in his sore arm. The outlaw still managed to hold onto the gun and finish pulling it from the holster. He lifted and shot again.

Sam also shot a second time. Flaming death belched from the gun barrel. That bullet hit Fisk directly in the heart, sending a geyser of blood streaming from the outlaw's chest. Fisk took a step forward and fell to the ground, still holding the gun in his hand. He twitched and then lay still.

Sam walked over to the body, briefly examined it. By the door, a group of men were talking. As Sam got closer, he noted that Delgado was addressing Holz and Easton. Some of the Mexican soldiers were retrieving the horses.

"You all know what this means," Delgado said. "I had been willing to negotiate in good faith, since my main concern is peace and harmony with my northern neighbors. But this changes everything."

"In what way?" Easton demanded. "There was no attack made on your life. It was Sam Two-Wolves this outlaw was after."

"No matter. The way I look at it, if you have such lawlessness in your own country that you cannot control it, why should you be allowed in my country? No, gentlemen, we will take care of our problems in our own way."

"You are not being reasonable!" Easton said.

"And if you allow any of your American so-called law enforcement officers across the border, it will be an international incident, one which your superiors in Washington will hear about. Be warned." Delgado then nodded at Leeds. "It was an excellent meal, Colonel. My compliments to the cook!"

He then turned and rode off without another word.

Fourteen

Ben and Tom got away from San Angelo without any problem. Nobody tried to stop them or gave chase. Along the way, nobody recognized them or threatened them. After several hours, the two started to relax. Their horses waded across the Rio Grande without incident. They followed the main trail and stopped at a cantina. They had only a little money between them, but it was enough for a few beers and some beans.

"This was easier than I expected," Tom said. "That was the best jail I've ever been in—it was the easiest to get out of! Wonder if Fisk had luck as good as ours."

"Who cares? Far as I'm concerned, he's going to get what he deserves. I'm more concerned now about us. We're here, but now what? Down to our last dollar. We're wanted back in the States. And we have information for Dingo Whaley, and have no idea where to find him."

"You really haven't been around that much, have you?" Tom asked. "A man like Whaley might be able to hide from the law, but word gets out . . . if you know who to ask."

"He's not exactly going to hang a sign out advertising his hideout."

"No, but he has money that he will spend. He is involved in various jobs that those in the know will hear about. Give me an hour, and I bet I can narrow the search down. Maybe even find out where he's holed up."

Ben reached into his pocket. He said, "After I pay for this meal, I'll have a dollar left. If you can find Whaley by this afternoon, I'll give you this dollar."

"It's a deal. Be ready to part with your money."

Tom sauntered out of the cantina and out back, as if to relieve himself. When he saw he was alone, he pulled off his boot and slipped his fingers through a slit in the lining, pulled out a small wad of bills. This stash was a secret he shared with nobody. He had learned from experience that ultimately nobody was trustworthy, and that a little backup cash was indispensable.

He counted out one hundred dollars. It

174

wasn't much, but it would be enough to put him in the position to find out what he needed to know.

This town wasn't much—a few adobe houses, cantinas, stables. It didn't take Tom long to find what he was looking for behind one of the stables. Several men, Mexican and American, were crouched down in the dirt shooting craps. Tom knew that in every town there was at least one continuous game going on and the players would be the kind of men he could deal with on equal terms. He also kneeled, threw some money down. He didn't have to say a word as the dice were passed to him.

The stakes were not high. He won a little, lost a little more, and the players opened up to him.

"You just passing through?" a bearded American asked.

"Maybe. Depends on what I find. I've heard things."

"We all hear things."

"But what I've heard could be of particular interest to a certain person."

"Talk straight."

"I've got information for Dingo Whaley. It's about one of his men. Mel Murdock."

"Roll the dice." Tom tossed the dice, lost a little more. "He and his gang have been hanging around San Jacinto, where the Mex Army has an outpost. It's not that far from here—if you really want to look him up."

"Why wouldn't I?"

"Haven't you heard about Whaley? He's a mean SOB. Never know what he's going to do. He just about beat a poor bartender to death for not bringing a beer fast enough. He's not somebody I'd want to cross paths with for any reason."

"He'll want to know what I have to tell him."

"Maybe. I still wouldn't take the chance of getting killed. But it's your skin."

Tom handed the dice back to the other man.

"Believe it's your turn to roll."

The bearded man squinted his eyes and said, "You ain't no lawman. I knew that before you even hunkered down to play. But to show you how slick Whaley is, he's even got the local military to keep their hands off him. He's got a sweet deal. But I wouldn't want any part of it."

"Thanks for the advice. I'll keep it in mind."

The gold arrived in San Angelo later than expected. It was after dark and was received with little fanfare, since Finch wanted as few

176

people as possible to know about the gold. Unfortunately, it was almost impossible to keep secrets in a small town like San Angelo.

Finch and Leeds supervised the movement of the gold into the safe. The guards that came with the gold were used, and then were positioned throughout the town to be available if needed.

"Bad break about your dinner," Sam said to Leeds as the last bars were placed and the safe door closed. "None of us expected Fisk to come gunning for me like that. I would never have thought it of him."

"Like I've said before, there's no telling what a man will do."

"Still, the way Delgado walked out . . ."

"Delgado didn't want to negotiate in good faith," Leeds said. "He was interested only in making himself seem reasonable. What he really wanted was an excuse to continue what he's already been doing . . . and to make us look like the bad guys. I'm not sure if Easton and Holz fell for it or not. On the other hand, they can always say they tried and Delgado is being unreasonable. Who knows?"

Finch stepped up, pounded Leeds on the shoulder.

"Hey, heard the good news about you and Rosie! Congratulations!"

"So you actually popped the question?"

Matt asked. "You do like to live dangerously! And she agreed to your demands?"

"She said 'Yes!'" Leeds said. "You'll understand someday, Matt. There'll come a time when you'll want more from life than wandering and excitement."

"I can't see it coming for a long, long time."

"Trust me. It'll happen."

"What if you get a promotion?" Sam said. "She willing to go with you?"

"And leave this all behind?" He laughed. "She'll be by my side from now on. And I couldn't be happier."

"Then we'd better make sure that another fiasco doesn't happen like last night," Finch said. "Matt, Sam, you take your positions as we discussed. I'm going over to keep track of Murdock. We may have to wait for a few hours or several days. So let's get started."

Ben and Tom entered the outskirts of San Jacinto. To them, the town looked about the same as the others they had passed through, except that it did have a fortlike building in its center.

"You got my last dollar," Ben said. "But if your friend gave you the wrong direction, I want my money back!"

"No. That's a done deal. I think that Whaley is probably here. It's still a matter of looking in the right place."

"Better do it pretty soon. I'm getting hungry. And we still don't have any guns. I'm not too keen on spending another night outside with not even a blanket."

"Just stay calm. I'll handle it."

"You think so? Well, you're not the only person that can find somebody. Watch this!"

"Please . . . don't."

Ben ignored Tom's plea as he went up to a group of men around a water trough, talking to themselves.

"Hey, men!" Ben said. "We're looking for somebody. Maybe you can help us?"

"Yeah? Who you looking for?"

"Man named Dingo Whaley."

"And why would you be looking for him?"

"We have information that he'd be interested in. We want to tell him personally—"

Ben was interrupted by a large-caliber handgun stuffed into his guts.

"How bad you want to see Whaley?"

"Ummm . . . pretty bad."

"Off the horse." Another man pulled Tom roughly off his horse. "I'll take you both to him. I'll warn you, he might not like to be interrupted. You still want to meet him?"

"Well," Tom said. "It could wait . . ."

The men pushed Tom and Ben in front of them toward the fortlike structure. "Too late for that. You wanted to see Whaley. You'll see Whaley. It might be the last thing you ever see, unless you tell one helluva story."

"Why don't you do the talking this time," Ben muttered.

"I think that'd be a wise idea."

Delgado, seated at his desk, laughed as he told the story to Whaley.

"You should have seen the look on the official's face when I told him I couldn't deal with a country that couldn't even enforce its own laws!" Delgado said. "And when I informed them that I would arrest any of their law officers that stepped foot on Mexican soil . . . the moment was priceless! Perhaps the high point of my career!"

Whaley smiled. "Yeah, that would've been worth seeing! But I don't imagine you called me here to tell me these stories—as funny as they are."

"That is correct. I have some information for you. I took the opportunity of my visit to verify some information I had received from other sources. The gold you are interested in is to arrive tonight. It is supposed to be a secret. But you know about secrets."

"Perfect! I'll have my men together and ready to ride."

"One of your men is also being held in the same fort. A man named Mel Murdock."

"Murdock. He's a joke. We left him behind, hoping they'd kill him. Guess we didn't get lucky, after all."

The talk was interrupted when Pierce entered the cantina, pushing two other men in front of him. They looked like small-time hoods to Whaley and were of no concern to him.

"What's with this trash?" Whaley asked.

"These two jokers were asking about you around town. They said they have some information for you."

"Today must be your lucky day," Delgado said.

"So you brought them to me? What information could they have that would interest me?"

"We've just come in from San Angelo." Tom was speaking fast. "We've got information about one of your men. Mel Murdock."

Whaley rolled his eyes toward the sky. "How long must I keep hearing about Murdock? I would have been better off shooting him myself!"

"He's being held by the authorities up at Fort Concho," Tom continued.

"So is that my concern?"

"He's getting preferential treatment. We've seen it with our own eyes. And do you know why?"

Whaley leaned forward, elbows on the table, holding a glass in his hands.

"Please. Do tell me."

"Because he's squealing on you. He's turned on you, testifying against you in return for a lighter sentence. They offered us the same kind of deal."

Whaley's hands suddenly grew white. He slammed the glass to the table, shattering it against the wood.

"What difference does it make?" Delgado asked conversationally. "You're in Mexico now. They can't touch you. Why worry about it?"

"Because I don't like anybody going against me. More importantly, I don't like Murdock. We'll just have to teach him a lesson. And give the message to anybody else that is thinking about crossing Dingo Whaley."

He looked up, saw Tom and Ben still standing quietly before him.

"You two are still here?"

"We were thinking . . . well . . . maybe you could use our help . . . that is, let us join your gang . . ."

"You think your information was that valuable?"

Tom gulped. Nothing ever seemed to work out for him like it was supposed to. He took a deep breath and continued talking. "We could help your men in lots of ways. We know the layout of Fort Concho. We know where Murdock is being held. We could help guide you."

"And I'm good with explosives," Ben suggested. "You get me the dynamite, and I can guarantee an explosion right where you want it."

"I don't like partial measures. How about leveling the entire building? While on the back of a running horse?"

"If that's what you want . . . that's what I'll do."

Whaley leaned back in his chair. "Then maybe you two can be of help, after all." He asked Delgado, "How are you with supplies of dynamite? Think you could spare a few sticks?"

"A box or two," Ben suggested.

"That could be arranged," Delgado said. "When would you like it?"

"Let's strike while the iron is hot. We'll be there tomorrow night. We'll hit them before they know what's happening."

"Then let's do it. Revenge and gold. Killing two birds with one stone. I like it. I like it a lot."

Mary called out softly, "Sam! It's me! Can I come in?"

Sam rose and unlatched the door. Mary walked in, carrying a basket and a pot of coffee.

"I'm not complaining, mind you, but this is supposed to be kind of a secret," he said.

"I won't tell anybody. And nobody saw me come here. I pretended like I'm bringing this to the colonel for a snack. Besides, you've been here for a very long time. I thought you could use some help."

"This is luxurious compared to some places I've been . . . but, thank you. That is very considerate of you."

She put the basket down softly.

"Will you hold me? I feel very alone." The request startled Sam, but he allowed the woman to come sit next to him on the floor. He put his arm around her and held her close.

"What's the problem? I'm listening."

"Rosie is going to marry the colonel. They will probably move away, sooner than later. Rosie has been like a big sister to me. When she moves away, I will have nobody."

"I never thought of that," Sam admitted. "I'm really happy for Leeds and for Rosie. It could be a bum deal for you. Maybe I could talk with Leeds . . ."

"No, that's not what I want. I don't know what I want, exactly. I know you're not the man for me. You're not ready to settle down . . . you may never be. But you are special and I wanted to spend at least a little time with you before you go. Can you understand that?"

"You flatter me. You deserve the best. Wish I could give it to you."

Sam kissed her softly. Mary returned the kiss hungrily. Sam considered making another move, when she put her head on Sam's shoulder and sighed.

"Thank you, Sam. For listening." She stood up, straightened her skirt. "Take care, Sam. Please . . . take care."

Fifteen

Matt's job was to help patrol the area out-side the fort. It was better than being stuck inside for an indefinite period of time, as Josiah and Sam had been, but there was no guarantee he would be in on the action when it started. Some soldiers were patrolling other parts of San Angelo, but there was always the possibility that the Whaley gang could sneak into town undetected. Or maybe they wouldn't show at all, in spite of the gold and the prisoner being used as bait.

As Josiah said, nothing in life was certain. And it was a plan. If it didn't work, all they had lost was a little time. If it did work, they would have the Whaley gang in custody. It was worth the gamble.

Even so, the gang would have to make its move soon. The gold would have to be used as payroll and Murdock would have to go to trial. Time was running out. When that happened, some tough decisions would have to be made about crossing the border after the outlaws. It could mean defying the governments of two different countries. It wasn't a decision that Matt was looking forward to making.

He rode slowly, keeping off the main road. Much traffic passed through San Angelo for it to be such a small community: the stage line, hunters, soldiers, cowboys, and drifters. Even now, after dark, there was a steady stream of people entering and leaving the city. Matt watched them all in silence, waiting for something to happen.

Inside the fort, Sam continued to sit with his back to the wall so that he could keep in view the window, door, and safe. He would be able to see anybody trying to get in before they could do serious damage. He figured that when the Whaley gang made their move, they would come into town quietly and try to kill Murdoch and take the gold with as little fanfare as possible. After all, why would they be interested in a full-fledged gunfight?

Sam's mind, however, kept drifting to Mary's kiss. She was warm and willing. Had he pushed a little more, she would have given herself to him. Yet, he had not pushed. Instead, he had let her talk and then return to the cantina, leaving the basket of food behind. Perhaps it was because Sam knew something of loneliness. He had a few friends, and he was closer to Matt, his blood brother, than most people could ever imagine. Still, he was essentially a loner. He had lost his parents. He never stayed in one place for very long at a time. He had no wife, and no plans to look for one. There were times when he thought about a different life—one like Mary had talked about—and he understood.

Because of that, he could not take advantage of her. She would eventually find the life she wanted. Sam felt it would not be fair to make an implicit promise that he could not fulfill, so he let her walk away.

Still, he remembered how her body had felt against him and the scent of her hair when her head rested on his shoulder.

The room suddenly felt small and confined. Sam stood, walked around to stretch his legs, glanced out the window to see if anything was out of the ordinary. So far, only the usual crowds of people were out and about.

Sam returned to his position to continue his patient wait that might or might not lead to something.

* * *

Mary was taking a break from her duties at Rosie's. She dried her hands on a towel as she leaned against the wall of the cantina. Her mind was not on her job. Instead, she was thinking about Sam and their brief talk earlier in the day.

Why hadn't Sam made a play for her, as so many other men did? He had been a perfect gentleman. He made her feel like she was somebody important, not just a barmaid in a tiny Texas town. He had talked to her as a person, somebody whose thoughts and feelings mattered.

And maybe they did. Mary was losing her friend and teacher, but that didn't necessarily mean that she no longer had a future. After all, Mary thought, if Rosie could pull herself up from her humble beginnings and move up in the world, so could she! Sam had helped her to see that, whether he realized it or not.

She daydreamed for a few minutes longer, enjoying the cool night air. She thought of Sam cooped up in that little room and wondered if she could visit later in the evening. This time, she perhaps would not leave so soon. Sam surely wouldn't be mad about that?

Her thoughts were interrupted by the sound of a dozen or more horses. They were coming in fast. In seconds, they came into

189

sight, headed straight for the area of the fort where the prisoner, Murdock, was being held.

Whaley and his gang planned simple, direct action: Move in fast, move in hard. Don't try anything fancy with Murdock, just dynamite the jail cell into rubble. Don't try to finesse the gold, just dynamite the building, grab the gold, and get out. Make it like an old-fashioned military raid: no prisoners, just destruction.

Jessup primarily organized the group with Ben's help in arranging the explosives. With such a simple plan, there wasn't a whole lot that needed to be arranged. In addition to the mounted riders, they brought along several horses to carry the gold. Delgado was generous with the dynamite, which was packed on two additional horses. It was enough explosives to do the job and then some. It was more dynamite than Ben had ever seen at one time in his life. It was strangely exciting to him.

As the arrangements were being made, Tom felt almost like an outsider. He didn't look or act like the other members of the gang. He didn't have the expertise to contribute as Ben did. Most of the others ignored him as they got their own horses and gear ready.

Tom felt even more out of place as the gang saddled up and were on their way. They all rode together as a team, occasionally talking among themselves. Pierce handled the extra horses. Ben handled the horses with the dynamite. Tom had nothing to do but try and keep up.

It was nearly dark as they reached San Angelo. The group stopped briefly to compare notes.

"Tom, you bring us to the jail first. Ben, blow the hell out of that place. And do it fast." Ben retrieved several sticks of dynamite from the packs and wired them together. "Then go for the gold. If anybody moves, shoot them. You all know your jobs. The rest of us will provide cover. Now *go!*"

Ben had never fought in a war, but as he rode toward the town with the others he thought this must be how it felt to ride into battle, a part of a group that knew how to get results. The night wind blew against his face, the horse was strong beneath him, the dynamite was solid in his hand.

Soon, they had entered the town and were passing the adobe houses and cantinas to the fort. Ben found the small window with bars

191

where Murdock was being held and lit the fuse of the dynamite.

Josiah Finch sat in a straight-backed chair leaning against the wall just outside the jail cell where Murdock was being held. A shotgun was across his lap.

"You've been guarding me for days," Murdock said. "You know something I don't? Think maybe Whaley's going to try and spring me?"

"You tell me. Are you that valuable to the gang?"

"Yeah. I was one of the main guys. They couldn't do without me."

"They've stayed pretty busy without you since my boys brought you into custody. If you were so important, why'd they leave you behind to start with? Why haven't they come after you sooner?"

"Hell, Whaley's a busy man. They must have you worried. Or why'd you be watching over me like a mother hen?"

"I've heard the rumors that you sold out Whaley. That you are working with me to put together a case against Whaley."

Murdock's face turned white. "But that ain't true!"

"You have talked with me. And that is what

the rumors have said. I imagine that'll get back to Whaley, and he'll come to take care of the situation."

"You set me up!" Murdock said.

"Just used you to help bait the trap," Finch corrected. "The idea is to bring them to us."

"Anyway, Whaley's too smart for that," Murdock said. His voice was less certain. "He wouldn't fall for that trick. Would he?"

"You know him better than I do. You know how crazy he gets sometimes. Or so I've heard. Is that true, as well?"

"You don't want to cross him," Murdock said, rubbing his face.

"So what do you think?"

"He'll be here. I just hope you got a big enough gun to protect me." He moved as far from the window as possible. "There's no telling what Whaley will do."

"When he gets here, I'll be waiting for him . . ."

Suddenly the world exploded. Josiah Finch saw the outside wall of the jail cave in before he heard the sound of the explosion. Rubble fell into the cell, covering Murdock. Had he stayed next to the window, he would have been crushed.

Finch was instantly in action. He fell to the floor, caught a rider in his sights through the new hole in the wall, and shot. Both barrels belched flame and one of the riders fell to the ground. Finch couldn't see through the dust who he had hit.

Several men started to fire through the hole. Finch shot back, blindly, and then reloaded the shotgun.

One of the riders moved in close holding several sticks of dynamite wired together with a short fuse. He tossed it through the hole into the cell.

Finch dived for cover, but it was too late as the second explosion filled the room with a deafening roar. To Finch, the next seconds seemed like hours. Like a bad dream, he could see the sharp piece of wood flying at him, but he could not move fast enough to get out of the way. He saw the chunk bury itself in his shoulder like some wooden sword and felt the blood wet his shirt.

From overhead, several beams started to fall. Josiah tried to roll to one side, but the pain in his shoulder slowed him down. The large pieces of wood hit him a glancing blow on the side of his head and then across his back. He managed to crawl the final few feet through the rubble to the street before he finally collapsed, unconscious.

* * *

Mary watched the riders, but thought little about them at first. San Angelo was always being visited by such men as these. Though they would often shoot up the town, the damage was seldom permanent.

These riders, however, made her nervous as she thought about Sam waiting in his small room. Would the men he was waiting for be as bold as this? Could it be the Whaley gang? The answer came soon in the form of an attack and explosion on Murdock's cell.

She dropped her towel and ran toward the fort where Sam was holed up. She had to warn him! And she had only minutes . . . maybe seconds.

Mary burst into the room only seconds after he heard the huge explosion from down the street. Only Sam's quick instincts and training kept him from shooting.

"They've dynamited the jail! It's gone . . . totally gone! Get out, they'll be here next!"

The sound of hoofbeats outside came through the window. Sam knew Mary was telling the truth and that the Whaley gang was more crazed than anybody could have guessed. They weren't out just to silence Murdock and take the gold, they wanted to level the town.

"Get out of here," Sam hollered, pushing Mary in front of him. "Get out, now!"

The two made it out the door just as Ben rode up under cover of gunfire and tossed another huge bunch of dynamite wired together against the outside wall. That explosion was even louder than the one that had leveled the jail. Wood and adobe rained down on Sam and Mary.

He pushed Mary to the ground and covered her with his body as another explosion, this one at the safe itself, filled the air. Chunks of metal flew through the air. One nasty piece hit Sam in the back of the head, though he had managed to protect Mary from most of the force of the attack.

In seconds, Whaley's gang was inside the open safe. They efficiently gathered together the gold and placed it in bags, which they loaded on the spare horses.

From up and down the street a few soldiers were shooting, but they had no clear view of the enemy, and at the moment they were outnumbered by the guns of Whaley's gang.

In less than five minutes, the gold had been cleaned out; then another figure came racing down the street. The gunfire from Whaley's men slowed him down, but could not stop him. The men still on the ground quickly got back in their saddles.

"Good job, men!" Whaley called out. "Now let's get out of here!"

The outlaws raced south, guns banging behind them, discouraging pursuit.

Matt was just outside town when he heard the first explosion. He knew that he could not monitor every entrance into town, but he was still angry that the Whaley gang had made it past the soldiers that had been positioned along the way.

He spurred his horse back toward the fort. The first sight he saw was the area that had housed the jail cells, reduced to rubble. He then saw Josiah Finch lying in the street, a piece of wood sticking out of his shoulder. He stopped, found Josiah was still breathing. He spotted a cowboy hiding behind a horse trough and ordered, "Get the post doctor. Pronto! If he's not here in five minutes, I'll track *you* down. Got it?"

The cowboy nodded his head, and Matt was back on his horse when he heard the second explosion.

Hot lead met him as he raced down the street. He fired in the direction where he thought the shots were coming from, but his progress was slowed by the bullets.

When he found Sam, barely conscious, Matt reacted like a wild man. He ran into the building, guns blazing, indifferent to any danger to himself.

By this time, the gold had all been moved and the last outlaw was getting back in the saddle and racing into the night. Matt could have given chase, but he had other priorities.

He kneeled by Sam, who groaned and touched the back of his head.

"I'm all right," he said. "Don't let them get away. Those bastards are crazier than any of us thought. We can't let them get away with this."

"We'll get them later," Matt whispered. "Right now, we have other things to worry about. Josiah's been hit."

Sam shook his head to clear it and was on his feet.

"Where is he? How bad is he hurt?"

"I called for the doctor. He should be at the doctor's office by now. Which is where you should be, as well. Have that bump on your head looked at."

"Don't worry about me, I have a damned hard head," Sam said, helping Mary to her feet. "We miscalculated this time. But Mary warned me. She may have saved my life."

"Thank her later. Let's go take care of Josiah."

Sixteen

Matt and Sam knew they should be following Dingo Whaley's gang and the gold they had stolen. Maybe that was what Texas Rangers should have done. But the two blood brothers were friends to Josiah Finch before anything else, and they wanted to make sure he would be taken care of. They had carried the little Ranger to the doctor's office on a stretcher and waited while the physician looked him over.

Both men were so angry that they spoke little as they sat and paced in the darkened room. Dr. Stanford worked in the adjoining room, lit with kerosene lamps. The light shined through a crack between the bottom of the door and the floor. Movement could be heard, but Matt and Sam could see nothing.

"Maybe we shouldn't wait around for Stanford to be finished," Matt said. "Maybe we should go after Whaley?"

"We'll pick up the trail. Sometimes patience is a virtue. Remember what you learned growing up in my father's camp."

"I know. I'm usually as patient as any Cheyenne. But right now I'd like to get my hands on Whaley and his men . . ."

"We will. You can count on it. We will."

Matt touched the gun on his hip. He said, "Yes. We will."

The door finally opened and Stanford stepped through. He lit a lamp on the wall and sat down across from Matt and Sam. He was a graying man that served as the doctor at Fort Concho.

"Your friend is one tough bird," Stanford said. "He got hit in the head with something—a piece of wood, I guess—that would have killed most men. He's got a pretty-good-sized bump, and right now he's unconscious, but he's alive. I also dug out a large shaft of wood that had been forced into his shoulder by the explosion. He lost some blood, but I imagine he'll regain full use of his arm. Otherwise, he experienced some cuts, scrapes, and bruises."

"How about the other man?" Sam asked. "The one that Josiah was guarding. Murdock."

"He's alive, but in a lot worse shape than your friend. I'm not sure he'll make it."

"Thanks, Doc."

"I'll check Finch's progress through the night. You don't have to worry about him. I suppose you're now going after the men that did this?"

Matt concluded, "If Josiah wakes up before we get back, give him the message. We'll get the job done for him—no matter what it takes."

Matt and Sam spoke softly as they left the doctor's office. "We *will* get Whaley's bunch," Sam said grimly. "It's now a personal matter. And we will get them, no matter how long it takes or where we have to go. Nobody is going to stand in our way."

"You need sunlight to cut their trail?"

"Nope. You and I both know where they're going. I'd wager any amount of money that they're headed straight for Mexico. In fact, I'm so sure of it that I advised Colonel Leeds to station some of his men down by the river, just in case they escaped from the trap we set for them up here."

"Not a bad idea," Matt said. "Though I doubt the colonel's men have enough grit to actually stop them."

"But it might slow them down," Sam said.

* * *

Whaley led his men through the night. He didn't bother taking back trails. He just ran the horses as fast as they could go, and made good time in spite of the gold on the backs of some of the horses. He sent a few of his men ahead, to scout out the area for potential problems.

Almost to the border, Whaley stopped his men for a brief rest when Jessup flagged them down as he returned from his scouting mission.

"The bluecoats are trying to play it smart," Jessup said. "They have soldiers posted at many of the crossings. Including the one up ahead, where we were going to cross."

"How many guards?"

"Only a few men at each place. Mainly kids. They could still be a problem. I've got some alternate routes laid out where they don't have any men . . ."

"Nope. We're not changing the plan."

"Like I said, they have guards posted . . ."

Whaley's voice grew soft. "Are you questioning my decision?"

"No . . . no."

"Good. Have Pierce and a few others get out their buffalo guns. Take the soldiers out and we'll be able to cross without any problem. Understand?"

"Yes."

"Good. Do it. Now."

It didn't take long for Jessup to gather together Pierce and two others and make it to the ridge overlooking the river crossing. Below, three soldiers thought they were hidden behind stunted trees. But they were young and inexperienced. They didn't realize that they made clear targets in the starlight.

"This is almost too easy." Pierce laughed. His voice seemed to cut through the night.

"I don't know," Jessup said. "This doesn't feed right to me."

"What, you getting pansy-assed in your old age?"

"I don't know. Maybe it's like you said. Maybe it's too easy."

"Then let's make it more of a challenge." Pierce stood up and yelled out, "Hey, you down there! Yeah, you clowns by the river!"

The soldiers jumped, guns ready, looked around for the voice.

"Pierce, what are you doing?"

"Making a challenge of it!" he answered. "Hey, you clowns, up here!"

Finally locating the source of the voice, one of the soldiers lifted his gun, but not soon enough. Pierce's gun boomed. The heavy slug lifted the soldier off his feet and slammed him into the river.

The second soldier returned the fire and

dived for cover. Jessup's big gun then exploded, sending death into his chest. He fell back against the tree and slumped to the ground.

Pierce's gun shot again, and the third soldier went down.

"Well, that was easy," Pierce said. "Let's meet up with Whaley."

"They'll have some way to keep in contact with each other," Jessup said. "When they don't receive word, they'll find the bodies."

"And we'll be in Mexico by then," Pierce said. "Nobody can touch us there. Don't worry about it."

Colonel Elvin Leeds felt good. He had been on horseback for hours, leading his men from Fort Concho to the Mexican border, issuing orders and arranging them in the way that he felt they would be most effective. It felt good to be in the saddle, riding through the night like he used to do. Though he had never gotten away from it, the paperwork had been taking up more and more of his time—more than he had realized, until now.

On the other hand, he had gotten more used to being at a desk for most of the day, and the ride had left him a little sore. Maybe it was time for him to seriously consider looking for that promotion.

Lack of men was always a problem for the army, and this was no exception. He knew from experience that there was no way to patrol the entire Rio Grande. No matter how careful the planning, there were too many ways in which a determined man or group of men could slip across the border. Leeds had positioned his soldiers at most of the main crossings that he knew about, and a few that were not as well-known. It was the best he could do. He hoped that the plan developed by Josiah, Matt, and Sam would work and the soldiers would not be needed.

Leeds was now riding from one checkpoint to his main base of operations, though it was nothing special. It was only a campfire around which some of his men were sitting, along with two "guests" he would have just as soon left behind. Throughout the night, messengers from each of the various positions would report in to him at this camp, grab a cup of coffee and a little grub, then return to their posts. It was a primitive means of communication, but it would do the job.

Peter Easton and Carl Holz stood as Leeds rode up to the fire.

"Gentlemen," Leeds said. "The men are all in position."

"I still don't understand what the point of all this is," Holz said. "We don't know that the Whaley gang is going to show up in San Angelo. We don't know that they are going to attack anybody or anything. This seems like a waste of federal dollars."

"With all due respect, I am still in charge of military operations, and this is my call."

"Don't mind him," Easton said. "I know how difficult it is for you military men to take orders from civilians. I also know that you understand your limitations—based on the law."

"I understand. And I will follow the law, no matter how much it may pain me. Knowing, as we all do, that it benefits that Delgado fellow down south more than it does us."

"We all have our jobs to do," Holz said. "You just do yours and we'll be OK. And your job is not to question policy."

Leeds thought, *Maybe I can get in the position where I can have a say in policy.* For now, however, he did have his job to do.

Each station reported in as scheduled, except for the three men at the crossing about six miles downriver. They were late enough that Leeds was considering sending out his own messenger to check it out when the next rider galloped into camp. He rode past Holz and Easton, straight to Leeds.

"Sir. I have news. And it's not all good."

"Let's hear it," Leeds said in a grim voice.

Easton puffed out his chest as he listened. Holz paced back and forth.

"The Whaley gang attacked last night in San Angelo, just as the Rangers said they would," the soldier said. "Josiah Finch was injured. The other two, Matt Bodine and Sam Two-Wolves, stayed behind to take care of Finch."

"What about the gang?"

"They apparently got away."

Leeds had a bad feeling about the men that had yet to report in. "Grab a cup of coffee, then report back here in five minutes. I'm going downriver to check on some of my men who have not reported in. I need some assistance."

"Right away, sir."

The soldier saluted and walked to the fire, leading his horse behind him.

"We're going with you, Colonel," Easton said.

"Do as you want. I really don't care. Just be ready to ride in five minutes."

Leeds issued several more orders, as his men jumped to attention and prepared to move.

Matt and Sam rode at a hellish pace for the second half of the night. Occasionally Sam would spot a sign indicating that they were going in the right direction, but most of the time was spent riding as fast as the horses could safely go in the dark. Whaley had put the gold on several horses that they had kept herded tightly together. It was faster going than a wagon would have been. Any traces of a trail was then lost in trampled ground where Leeds's men had also passed. Sam and Matt didn't slow down.

As dawn grew close, the two blood brothers were near the Rio Grande. They weren't concerned about looking for sign. They were certain that the Whaley gang was following the main trail, pushing as hard as they could. Matt and Sam were also pushing their horses faster than they would have liked, hoping to catch up to the outlaws before they reached the river.

"How many you figure there are?" Matt asked as they paused briefly to give their horses a rest.

"Maybe a dozen or more."

Matt patted his horse's neck, prepared to mount up again. "The river's just ahead. It's one of the main crossings. You think Whaley would go for such an obvious place?"

"Apparently. He's not even trying to throw us off the trail."

"I'd think Leeds would have some men there. It'd be nice to have Leeds as backup."

"It would be. But it's not necessary. We've both faced worse odds and come out ahead. It might even be better if Leeds wasn't there."

"I think he's a good man and a good officer, but we work better without a lot of interference. And then there's those political considerations. He's on our side, but with Easton and Holz breathing down his neck, his hands are tied. It could put him in an awkward position if we have to defy him. We'll do what we have to do. He'll understand that."

"He may understand that, but how will he respond? Will it be as Colonel Leeds, the officer of the U.S. Army? Or as Elvin Leeds, the man, the friend of Josiah Finch?"

The two men continued in silence. They moved more slowly now, more cautiously, not sure what they would find. They smelled the river. Then they heard the movement before they saw anything. It sounded like men moving in the shadows near the river, though they could not make out any details.

Matt went on one side of the trail and Sam on the other. Guns were drawn, senses were alert to danger.

The sun edged above the horizon, making clear the scene in front of them.

Colonel Leeds had his head bowed, as if in prayer, while his men stood in a semicircle around him. On the ground were three blood-splattered bodies.

Seventeen

Leeds had feared the worst, which was what he found when he arrived at the crossing where he had positioned his three soldiers. He had been in many battles with outlaws and Indians. He had seen men shot in half, hacked to death, and without their scalps. He had faced death and been wounded. Still, the idea of cold-blooded killing made him sick.

He knew the men were still green, but he hadn't expected them to fall so easily to the outlaw guns. Apparently they had been shot with large-caliber guns, with little more thought than if they were just animals. Two of the men had drawn their guns, and one had apparently managed to fire a shot, but it had done little good. All of the men were dead, killed with one shot each, and left to rot where they had fallen.

Easton's face showed concern as they followed Leeds to the site. Leeds dismounted and personally checked the bodies.

"Whaley's gang was here," he said. "Gentlemen, this is the kind of characters we are dealing with. To them international law means nothing. Human decency means nothing."

Holz turned green and slipped off his horse. He stumbled into the small bushes, where he got sick. Leeds ignored him and continued to examine his dead soldiers with professional competence.

"No need to call the surgeon," he said. "These men are all past help. Let's arrange them with at least a little dignity until we can get them back to the fort to make final arrangements."

"I'll help," Easton said.

Leeds glanced sharply at him, saw his overweight form and his soft hands. "*You* will help?"

"I know you all think I'm just a worthless bureaucrat, but in my younger days I served in the military. I've worked with fathers of men like these who have died in action. I'm not indifferent to their suffering."

"Maybe I misjudged you a little," Leeds said. "Sure, you can help."

It took several minutes to wrap the bodies

in blankets and arrange them in a line along the ground. The wounds were bad enough that blood continued to seep into the material in large splotches.

Holz stepped out from behind the bushes, looking pale. He said, "I'm . . . sorry."

"Never seen anything like this?"

"I've always spent my life in the classroom and behind a desk . . . this is all new to me . . ."

"It could be a lot worse. That's one reason that Finch, Bodine, and Two-Wolves are after these men."

"I suppose the Whaley gang . . . got away."

"They crossed the river and are in Mexico," Leeds said. "I'm sure of it. They killed these men like dogs and simply went across"—his voice grew sharp—"where, need I point out, we cannot reach them."

"What now?"

"Let's give these men a moment of silent prayer. Then I'll consider the few options open to us."

For a few moments, just before dawn, even the air seemed to grow still, as the men stood with bowed heads. That moment was short-lived as the sound of horses were again heard. Leeds and his men started to pull their guns, but the colonel motioned for his men to put them away as Matt and Sam rode into sight.

Their horses were tired, but they still kept their heads high, ready for more running, if needed. They joined the other men for a few more seconds of silence.

"Wondered when you two were going to show," Leeds said. "As you can see, the Whaley gang already passed by here."

"We followed them from town," Sam said. "We might have gotten an earlier start, but Josiah was injured . . . the doc says he'll be OK. We tried to catch up to them. Apparently we weren't in time to save these men."

"Nobody's to blame but the outlaws," Leeds said. "They were soldiers, doing their job. We'll get word to their families, if they have families, that they died doing their duty."

"The outlaws are in Mexico, now," Matt noted. "We'll be going after them."

"No," Holz said. "That will not be allowed."

Whaley and his gang had splashed across the river and were into Mexico before dawn. Once safely across, they slowed their pace. They laughed and joked at how easy it all had been. Whaley, feeling generous, sent word for Ben to ride up and join him.

"You did a good job, Ben!" Whaley said, pounding him on the back. "You took out that jail like a pro! We'll probably be able to use you again. You've earned a place with us! And I'll make sure you receive a bonus for this job."

Back with the others, Tom watched enviously as Whaley praised Ben.

"Looks like your buddy and Dingo are hitting if off!" Pierce said. He was riding beside Tom, leading one of the horses carrying the gold. "If Dingo likes you, he can be generous. If he doesn't like you . . . well, look at old Murdock."

"Why has he singled Ben out for praise?" Tom asked, more to himself than to anybody else. "It doesn't seem fair."

"Stay with us, and you'll learn quick that it's not fair that counts . . . it's what Dingo wants. If you want to keep on living, that is."

Tom said nothing more. He rode quietly, thinking about the unfairness of it all. It had been his idea, after all, to ride south and find Whaley after they had broken out of their cell in San Angelo. He was the one who had told Whaley about Murdock turning on him and providing evidence to the Texas Rangers. He was the one who should be rewarded, not Ben! He also knew that Pierce was right, and would not question Dingo Whaley's decisions.

About two hours into Mexico, Whaley caught sight of a detachment of Mexican soldiers, led by Delgado. Whaley neither sped up nor slowed his pace. He let Delgado come to him.

"Was your operation a success?" Delgado asked.

"Went off without a hitch," Whaley answered. "Took care of some personal business, got the gold, and got away without losing a single man. We'll divvy it up later, as agreed."

Delgado looked over the horses and men. He mentally estimated the amount of gold on the horses and the strength of the men compared to his own.

"I will do you the honor of providing an escort the rest of the way," the Mexican official said.

"You wouldn't be trying to say you don't trust us?" Jessup asked.

"Much could happen, even now. I want to make sure everything arrives safely."

"A deal's a deal," Whaley agreed.

"I will keep some of my men behind to watch your back trail," Delgado said. "I'm willing to bet all the gold on these horses that we'll have some uninvited visitors within the next few hours."

Whaley frowned.

"The army surely won't cross the river? You said in your meeting, that official, Easton, and

Colonel Leeds said the soldiers wouldn't cross. That was their orders."

"I'm not talking army," Delgado said. "I'm talking Matt Bodine and Sam Two-Wolves. I saw Two-Wolves in action. I heard about Bodine. They're crazy. If they decide to do something, they'll do it, come hell or high water."

"Nobody was following us."

"They'll be here."

"They're just two men. Let us at them, we'll bring them down to size."

"You may get your chance. For now, I'll leave some of my men behind. If they cross the river, I'll take them into custody. Maybe we can use them in some way. If not, we'll just have them killed. Either way, some time in our prisons might teach them the lesson they deserve."

Matt and Sam looked at Holz in disbelief.

"What did you say?" Matt asked, stepping forward with clenched fists.

"I said you will not be allowed to cross the Rio Grande into Mexico. That is the agreement we made with Mexican officials. Those are the orders from Washington."

"I think I'd like to wring your scrawny neck . . ." Matt said, approaching Holz. Leeds stepped between them. Matt paused.

"I'm sorry," Easton added. "In this case, Holz is right. My heart goes out to these dead men. I want to bring their murderers to justice. But we need to go through proper channels."

"Out of my way, Colonel," Matt said. "I intend to walk right over that pipsqueak. This is no longer just a matter of law. The Whaley gang almost killed our friend. It's now a matter of blood, even if it extends across the river. I'm not going to let anybody stand in our way."

"Just calm down," Leeds urged. "If you cross the river, you're not just breaking the law. You'd also be breaking the oath you took when you were sworn in as Texas Rangers. You cannot openly defy the laws of the United States and of Texas and still wear those badges."

Matt stepped back calmly. He unclenched his fists, reached up, and removed the badge from his chest. He threw it at Leeds, who caught it with one hand.

"In that case, here's my badge. I don't need it. I don't want it."

Sam followed suit. He pulled the badge from his shirt, tossed it nonchalantly at Leeds, who caught it with his other hand.

"I'm with Matt. I also resign. We can do

more good for Josiah, and for our country, as private citizens than as law officers."

"I'm sorry, but I can't allow it, even without your badges," Leeds said. "I also have my orders."

"If you still have ideas about slipping across, you cannot count on any help from the United States government," Easton said. "Neither we, nor the army, nor the diplomatic services, will be able to lift a finger to help you."

"Do you really think that bothers us?" Matt asked.

"My orders are also to try and stop you if you do try to cross," Leeds continued.

"In that case, then, I'm sorry . . ." Matt said as his fist lashed out faster than the eye could follow. He struck the side of the colonel's face, knocking him backward to the ground. In the same fluid motion, he leaned down, unsnapped Leeds's holster, and removed his gun, throwing it into the grass several yards away.

Sam at the same time pulled his gun and covered the other soldiers.

"Nobody move, and nobody will get hurt," he said. "We have no argument with any of you."

The others turned to Leeds, looking for

some kind of direction. He sat up, rubbing his cheek, looking dazed.

"Now you've really done it!" Holz yelled. "You've attacked an officer of the U.S. military! You're threatening civilians! You're . . ."

"Allow me," Sam said, as his fist lashed out. He didn't hit Holz hard enough to really hurt him, but it also sent him sprawling and shut him up.

The soldiers looked confused. Leeds motioned for his men to remain where they were.

"They've got the drop on us," Leeds said. "No use trying to stop them. No need for you all to get killed, as well."

"This makes you criminals!" Holz hollered up from the ground. "This makes you both outlaws just like Whaley and his gang!"

Matt had pulled his own gun and was stepping into his saddle. "In some parts of Texas, I could shoot you for that kind of insult," he said. "But you're too stupid to know that's an insult, so I'll let it go this time."

"If this makes us criminals, then that's the way it's going to be," Sam said.

"We'll be back with the prisoners and the gold . . . or we won't be back at all," Matt concluded.

Matt and Sam then kicked their heels into the sides of the horses, who sprinted with new energy. They splashed into the Rio Grande, the water kicking up behind and around them. The two ex-Rangers shot a few times over the heads of the soldiers, forcing them to hit the ground.

In minutes, the blood brothers had crossed to the other side and were racing away in clouds of dust. The soldiers leaped up and shot several times, though they didn't come close to hitting anything.

"That's enough, men," Leeds said. "There's no way we can stop them now. Let's get these dead soldiers back to Fort Concho."

Holz tried to clean the dust off his behind and told Easton, "Leeds could have stopped those men, if he had wanted to! He intentionally let those men across!"

"Seems to me that Matt and Sam had the upper hand," Easton said. "The colonel made a wise and prudent move."

"Don't tell me you're siding with these men . . . who are little better than the outlaws they're chasing! Do I have to remind you that both of our careers hinge upon the results of this mission?"

"And do I need to remind you that some things are more important than careers?"

"You may not care about your career, but I, for one, don't want to have my job jeopardized by the outlandish stunts of—"

"Shut up, Carl," Easton said. He turned away to watch the soldiers move the bodies.

Holz, still angry, pushed himself in front of Leeds. The colonel was still holding the two Texas Ranger badges that Matt and Sam had thrown at him.

"Colonel Leeds," Holz said. "Apparently my superior has gone as crazy as those two fools that just crossed the river. So I am taking matters into my own hands. I demand to know what you plan to do in regard to Matthew Bodine and Sam Two-Wolves breaking an unknown amount of laws in defiance of direct orders! What *do* you plan to do?"

"Wish them luck," Leeds said softly.

Eighteen

The sun beat down on Matt and Sam as they continued slowly along the trail in Mexico. The scenery was much the same as it was on the United States side of the river, though the trail was less traveled, making the tracks of the Whaley gang that much clearer. The horses, however, were tired. The two blood brothers stopped at a small hollow near a stream where the horses could drink, graze, and rest.

Matt and Sam took the opportunity to fill their own canteens and to check their guns and ammunition.

"Hope this doesn't take too long," Matt said. "We've got ammunition, and some food, but it might be hard to get new supplies down here."

"This could have stood some better planning," Sam agreed. "But we've got Yankee dollars, and that will be enough if we need new supplies. But we probably won't need them. We can move in fast, get the job done, and get back home. We'll have to play it by ear, but we've faced tougher challenges."

"I did hate to hit Leeds like that."

"I can't say the same about punching out Holz," Sam said. "I enjoyed that a lot. And Leeds will understand. You didn't hit him that hard."

"Still, we're completely on our own this time."

"Wouldn't have it any other way."

The two cinched their saddles and were about to be on their way again when they heard the telltale cocking of a gun. The hands of Matt and Sam each dropped to their holsters when a voice called out, "Do not move, else we will be forced to blow your heads off."

Sam's hand moved a fraction of an inch. The movement was greeted with the sound of a dozen other guns being cocked. Sam's hand froze.

From over the hill a dozen Mexican soldiers stood, rifles pointed at Matt and Sam. They slowly raised their hands. The soldiers separated to make way for a figure on horseback who rode down to the stream.

"Raul Delgado," Sam said in Spanish. "It is so good to see you again."

"Keep your pretty words, Sam Two-Wolves," Delgado said. "This is not a meeting of diplomats, as it was last time we met. You are now in my country. What are you two doing here?"

"Would you believe . . . sightseeing?" Matt asked.

"Always ready with a smart comment, aren't you? No matter. Maybe you are here on some kind of investigation? Perhaps you are after some outlaw? In any case, you are on Mexican soil without proper authorization."

"How do you know we don't have proper authorization?" Matt asked.

"Simply because I have not signed your papers. Therefore you have improperly and illegally crossed the border."

Matt turned to Sam and shrugged. "How do you like that? The colonel must have forgotten to send the papers?"

"Those damned bureaucrats. Can't trust them for a second, can you? Well, I'm sure Señor Delgado will help to correct that!"

"Of course I will help you. It will take some time, however, to straighten out this situation." He gestured to the soldiers. "Take them into custody . . ."

"Hold it," Sam said. "We'll be straight with you. We are in Mexico searching for some outlaws—the Dingo Whaley gang. They've committed numerous crimes across the border. We followed them here. They are all we are interested in."

Delgado put his chin in his hand and looked thoughtful. "Hmmm . . . Dingo Whaley? I've heard the name. You must want him very badly to defy your government to cross the border. Perhaps I can be of assistance." He paused, then added, "Of course, this might take even longer to straighten out. Until that time, consider yourself my prisoners."

Matt and Sam looked at each other, then at the dozen guns surrounding them. Now was not the time to fight. That time would come. Even so, they did not look up in time to see the soldier sneaking up behind them. With two swift blows the blood brothers were knocked unconscious.

Dingo Whaley and his men had not made it to the general headquarters of Raul Delgado. Instead, they paused at a small town along the way to rest and meet up with Delgado. Whaley had just sat down at a table and barely had time to finish his first beer when he heard his name called from outside the cantina.

"Damn." He looked around, but was temporarily alone. Not even the bartender was present. He decided to ignore the voice, took another drink. In a few moments, a soldier came into the room.

"Señor Whaley—the *comandante* requires your presence!"

"Tell him to go to . . . tell him I'll be there when I finish my beer."

Pierce, Jessup, Ben, and Tom entered as the soldier left.

"They're looking for you, boss," Pierce said. "They've got something interesting for you."

"What could possibly interest me now more than another beer . . . unless maybe a new girl . . ."

"They got Bodine and Two-Wolves."

Whaley put down the glass without finishing it. "That *is* news. Let's take a look."

Whaley stepped outside just as Delgado's men were placing Matt and Sam in an outbuilding near Delgado's quarters. The soldiers literally threw the two blood brothers into the building and locked the door.

"So that's the two Rangers that everybody's so upset about. Don't look so tough now."

"I've faced them," Tom said. "They're plenty tough. Don't underestimate them. Delgado's men must have gotten a lucky break. Those two Rangers won't let it happen again."

Delgado waved away the comment with a flip of his hand.

"With those two out of the way, we can now devote our time to more serious matters." Around the corner of the building a large wagon came into view, driven by two of the soldiers. "Let's specifically talk about the gold."

"The split was eighty-twenty, I believe," Whaley said.

"That was the figure agreed upon, but that did not include all the factors. There is the matter of storage, transportation, handling . . ."

"That was never brought up."

"It should have been. I want to make sure the gold arrives safely, where it can be counted, divided, and stored safely. I've already made arrangements for transportation and storage."

"So why the wagon?"

"This prison wagon has a false bottom. It is a perfect way to transport the gold without raising any suspicion."

"And move it to where?"

"To my main headquarters, as agreed."

"I'm not sure I trust you," Whaley said. "How do I know you're not going to try and sneak away part of the gold when we move it?"

"Why don't you have your men move it into the wagon. That way you can be sure that I will not cheat you."

"So we will. Pierce, get all the gang together. Take care of this. I'm getting another beer." He turned, then stopped. "And, Delgado, I'm having some of my men on the wagon as you transport the gold. Understand?"

"That will be no problem to arrange."

Sam woke first. He opened his eyes, felt the pain in the back of his head. This was the first time in years that he had been surprised in this way, and he didn't like it. That Matt had been caught in the same trap was little comfort. Both knew better. It wouldn't happen again.

Matt groaned slightly, just a few feet away. Sam, noting his hands were tied in front of him with a rough rope, crawled over to Matt. His hands were also tied.

"Hey, man, you all right?"

"Just feel stupid. How could we have let that son of a gun get the drop on us?"

"More importantly, how do we get out of this?"

They looked around and saw not a jail cell but a storage room. Sunlight streamed through the cracks in the shuttered windows.

"Think I'm insulted," Matt said. "They didn't even bother to put us in a jail cell."

Sam moved over to the window, looked through the cracks in the shutters. The bright sun hurt his eyes at first, but the pain in his head quickly faded away and he could focus once again on the scene outside.

"Don't get too insulted," he said. "I don't know where we're at, but I'd wager this town isn't big enough to even have a jail. Take a look. Other than a cantina and a church, doesn't look like this town has much of anything."

Matt joined Sam at the window in time to see Dingo Whaley and several of his men come out of the cantina.

"Well, look at that," Matt said. "Dingo Whaley himself. And with Delgado. No wonder he wasn't interested in helping us find the outlaw."

"He's in partnership with Whaley. Guess we should have guessed. They might have even had this whole thing arranged when Delgado was in that meeting with Easton and Holz. That SOB wasn't interested in striking a deal . . . he was up there to get more information about the gold shipment!"

"And to see how serious our government was about tying our hands."

"And they played right into their game. Damn." Sam rubbed his eyes. Though he could still see clearly, he had a dull throb in the back of his head. He was tired, and the blow to his head hadn't helped any. He hoped that it wouldn't hurt his quick draw, if it came to that.

"If we can get out of this, the information might prove interesting to Easton and his superiors in Washington," Matt said. "But the first thing is to find a way out of this." He stood, started to explore the room. It was full of boxes, bags of corn, and metal farm implements, including a plow hanging from the wall. He picked up a shovel, lifted it awkwardly with his tied hands.

"You'd make a good farmer," Sam joked. "You always did like to get down and dirty."

"Yeah, I'll need this shovel to scoop through the manure you toss my way!"

"As long as you keep your mind clean and pure . . . like mine!"

"I suppose your thoughts of Mary were pure as the driven snow!"

"Don't make fun," Sam warned. "That lady helped me out of a tight spot when Whaley's gang attacked San Angelo. I've had to change my mind about her." Matt started to come back with another insult, but Sam interrupted. "Come take a look at this."

Outside, a prison wagon had pulled up in front of the cantina. The horses used by the

Whaley gang, including those with the gold, were in a pen next to the cantina. All of the Whaley gang, except for Dingo himself, had gathered together and made a line from the pen to the coach. Then they started to remove the gold from the backs of the horses, passed it from man to man until it reached the wagon. The final man took the gold and did something with it inside the wagon. The vehicle was angled so that Matt and Sam could not see the side with the door, but they could figure what was happening.

"They're hiding the gold in the prison wagon," Matt said. "Why would they want to do that? Why not split it up now, if that's what they were going to do?"

"This is Delgado at work," Sam said. "It's not Whaley's style. This involves too many steps, and Whaley likes to keep things simple. Delgado's up to something."

"And take a look at the soldiers that are starting to gather. I'd say Whaley's in for a little surprise."

Whaley's men had worked up a sweat in the hot Mexican sun. Delgado watched patiently until the last gold bar was situated carefully. Whaley came out of the cantina to examine the work, half-full beer glass still in his hand.

The saddles and packs remained on the horses in the pen.

"Well, Señor Whaley, are you satisfied?"

"Jessup?"

"It's all there, boss. None of it is missing."

"Then I'm satisfied," Whaley said.

"And so am I. It is time." Delgado snapped his fingers, and soldiers suddenly appeared on the street, on the rooftops of the few buildings in town, and from behind the prison wagon. Whaley's gang members, tired from the physical labor, were confused at first as the soldiers made a circle around them.

"What is this?" Whaley demanded.

"I have given great thought to the situation," Delgado said, leaning against the wagon. "You have broken laws of your country, which is no concern of mine. But you have also broken many laws of my country. And I am sworn, after all, to uphold those laws."

Whaley's eyes narrowed. "I don't like the drift of your talk," he growled.

Delgado continued smoothly, "You are in this country illegally, of course. You have also attempted to bribe a federal officer. You were in possession of stolen property. I'm sure there are other laws that you violated. Give me a little time to think about it. I have no choice, therefore, but to place you and all of your men under arrest. And to confiscate the gold as evidence."

Whaley cursed, threw his glass at Delgado, and pulled his gun with the same motion. His men took the same cue. The soldiers shot, but either the guns were inaccurate or their aims were off, and most of the shots missed. One of Whaley's shots hit its mark, and a Mexican soldier fell to the ground.

Smoke filled the air. Whaley jumped the fence to the small corral adjoining the cantina and grabbed his horse. Others followed him, shooting at random into the pack of soldiers. Groans of pain mixed with the shots. Whaley's men furthest from the corral were not so lucky, as dozens of soldiers jumped on them and beat them to the ground.

Whaley spurred his horse and broke through the corral fence. He rode through the mass of men next to the prison wagon, followed by his men that were able to also grab a horse. Those not able to reach the corral in time were left behind.

Whaley shot one final time at Delgado, who slipped behind the wagon at the last second. The shot hit the wagon and bounced off one of the metal bars.

The soldiers fired at Whaley's gang, but they were already out of range.

Nineteen

In the locked shed, Matt and Sam watched the shooting through the cracks in the shuttered windows.

"A big surprise for Whaley," Matt said. "Now let's give Delgado a surprise." He jumped up, tested the metal plow hanging from the wall. "It's not as sharp as a knife, but it'll do." He sawed the ropes on the metal until they frayed and broke. With his hands now free, he loosened Sam's bonds.

"Now for some weapons," Sam said, looking around. "How are you with that shovel?"

"It'll let me clean up some of the dirt outside . . . if we can get the surprise on them," Matt answered.

"This ax handle will work for me. Until we can get some guns back."

"There's still horses in the corral. We can

grab a couple, get away, then come back for the gold. We'll worry about the Whaley gang when the time comes."

"Good plan."

Matt was already at the side door, pushing the shovel blade into the crack between the door and its frame. "This old shed wasn't built for security. It shouldn't take much to pry this loose."

Sam found a metal rod and inserted it in the bottom of the door and pried along with Matt. In seconds, the wood started to crack and then splintered. Matt pulled out the pieces of wood, tossed them to one side, and pushed open the door with his foot. The entrance was on the side of the building away from the street, and no guards had been posted. The two slipped out quietly, unnoticed in the noisy confusion going on across the road.

"Don't worry about Whaley!" Delgado said. "We have the gold. That's the most important thing. Put the prisoners in the wagon."

The members of Whaley's gang that had been captured continued to struggle, though they were outnumbered. Some blows with rifle butts finally quieted them down, though they remained conscious.

* * *

"I'm going to the roof," Matt said. "Get the drop on them."

"Oh, yeah, take the high ground, again!"

"Some of us are just destined for great heights. You can just jump in when the time looks right."

The adobe shed wasn't very high. Matt leaped and grabbed the roof, pulled himself up the rest of the way, taking his shovel with him. Below him, on the other side, the soldiers were bunched up around the prisoners, pushing them into the wagon. Dust and gunsmoke still filled the air, while some of the men tried to put the horses back in the corral and to repair the damage.

Matt took a breath and leaped, landing right in the middle of the soldiers. He held out the shovel horizontally so that the handle hit one soldier squarely in the back of the neck and the metal blade hit another soldier on the back of the head. Both went down before they knew what hit them.

Sam was suddenly also in the middle of the group. He seemed to be everywhere. He hit one soldier in the stomach with the end of the ax handle, doubling him up with pain. Sam pivoted, hit another soldier in the face, and kicked away the first soldier.

237

It took a few seconds for the remaining soldiers to realize what was happening. One tried to pull his gun. Matt's shovel came down hard. It landed with a bone-crunching whack, knocking the gun out of the soldier's hand, though it was unfortunately also out of Matt's reach.

The soldiers tried to move in on Sam, to overpower him as they earlier had the members of the Whaley gang, but Sam was ready for them. He swung his ax handle in a wide circle over his head and around him. The wood hit glancing blows off several of the attackers, leaving blood and torn flesh in its place. The assailants backed off. Sam knew, however, that was only a temporary reprieve. If they had enough space, they could use their guns and take him out easily. He needed a gun.

The entire fight so far had taken only seconds. Delgado watched in surprise. He had not considered the two Americans a serious threat, so had not taken enough precautions to secure them. Even so, he was amazed that they had already escaped and were making jokes out of his men.

He reached down to his belt, felt the guns taken earlier from Matt and Sam. They were state-of-the-art weaponry, the best money could buy, and in excellent shape. He had decided to keep them for himself. It amused him to think that the Americans could be killed with their own guns.

Delgado reached for the weapons.

Matt spotted Delgado around the side of the wagon, safely out of the fracas, and the movement of his hands toward the guns in his belt. Matt knew his gun like he knew his own hands, since it was almost a part of him. He figured that the other gun was Sam's.

Sam was clearing a large area around him, as Mexican soldiers lay stunned or bleeding on the ground and the ones still standing were backing away. Matt called out, "Sam! I'm coming through!"

Sam raised his ax handle in a higher arc. Matt dived, rolled safely beneath the swinging weapon, holding the shovel close to his body. On the other side of his blood brother, Matt reached out with his shovel, shoved it between Delgado's legs, and then rammed it straight up.

Delgado howled in pain.

Matt twisted the handle, causing Delgado to lose his balance. Sam jumped in, striking the Mexican across the chest, knocking him backward.

Matt plucked the guns from Delgado's hands and tossed Sam's gun to him. He fired at a soldier rushing him. The bullet hit with a solid smack, stopping him in his tracks. Sam leaped over him, hit the soldier at the gate with the butt of the gun, and grabbed his horse. He looked into the swirling group of horses, found Matt's, and grabbed the reins.

Delgado looked up at Matt from his position on the ground with hatred in his eyes. Matt slapped him softly on the cheek and said, "It was so nice of you to invite us for a visit. Too bad we can't stay. Maybe another time?"

In another instant, he was on the back of his horse. He and Sam were then racing out of town, the other horses in the corral following them in a large cloud of dust.

It took several minutes for the dust to clear and for Delgado to stop hurting. When he was finally able to stand, he was amazed at the wreck that Matt and Sam had left behind. Many of his men remained on the ground where they had fallen. Only a few horses were left, including the four-horse team hitched to the wagon.

Damn those Americans, he thought. *At least I still have the gold. I'll worry about those two later.*

A burly sergeant asked, "Orders, sir?"

"Get a group of men together and retrieve those horses," Delgado said. "Look around town, see if there are enough horses to mount a few guards to go with the wagon. I want it moved to my headquarters immediately, where the gold and the prisoners can be made secure. The rest of us can catch up later. Take a few men and search for those two Americans. I know they won't have gotten very far on tired horses."

"The Americans caught us by surprise," the sergeant continued. "If they try anything else, we'll be ready for them."

"Be prepared at all times. There's no telling where or when they'll show up next."

It was as if Matt and Sam had vanished into the Mexican countryside. The small search party wound up going in circles. They found the trail of what was left of Whaley's gang, but quickly lost all trace of Matt and Sam.

"I've heard lots of white folks say that 'no Indian can be found unless he wants to be found,' " Matt said softly. In the distance, the tired search party seemed to be wandering aimlessly. "I guess your father taught us well about how to disappear into the country."

"He taught us a great many things," Sam said, remembering the early days, before he promised his father to give up Indian ways for the life of a white man. "Like all great men, he probably taught us more than he—or we— realized at the time."

"Even a respect for life that most white men cannot understand," Matt said. "So many think that Indians count life as cheap, but that is actually not the case. We were taught to be ruthless in battle, but not to take life unless necessary. Those soldiers don't realize how close they are to death, if we chose to slip up on them with killing in mind."

"Letting them chase their own tails for a while is good enough," Sam agreed. "They'll give up the search, for now. Delgado will want to make sure the gold is safe before he goes after us or Whaley again. So I suggest we go after the gold."

"If we can get the prison wagon, we'd also have at least some of the Whaley gang, as well."

"Exactly."

In the distance, the search party looking for Sam and Matt were moving out again—in the wrong direction.

"They'll be busy for a while. Let's find that wagon."

"That won't be hard."

"Why? Because of your superior Native American tracking skills?"

"Naw. I just saw some of the wagon's tracks a mile or so back, when you were scouting in a different direction. The tracks were fairly fresh—no more than a few hours old. We'll just follow them and catch up in no time."

The prison wagon was moving slowly. The driver, a large man with a small mustache, was in no big hurry. He had gulped a few drinks at the cantina before taking his seat, and was now feeling relaxed. When he got home, his wife and seven kids would be waiting for him. All things considered, he liked where he was just fine and wasn't pushing any harder than necessary to keep Delgado happy.

A guard with a shotgun was sitting next to him on the high seat. Three other men rode in a wide circle around the wagon—one on each side and one to the rear. It was fewer guards than might normally be assigned for such a job, but most of the horses that had escaped from the corral were still missing and Delgado didn't want to delay the move any longer. It was a calculated risk, through he figured even these few men could even fight off what was left of Whaley's gang, much less the two Americans.

Matt and Sam followed the wagon at a safe distance, stirring up almost no dust. They determined that the guards were not communicating among themselves. They rode alone, sometimes barely within sight of each other. This would make it easier for Matt and Sam.

"I'll take the ones on the rear and the right," Sam said. "You take the ones on the left and on the wagon."

Matt nodded, and silently nudged his horse forward. Sam turned his horse toward his man.

Matt rode quietly, then increased his speed. Too late, the soldier sensed something behind him. He turned his head just as Matt vaulted out of his saddle, grabbing the soldier by the neck. The two fell to the ground, Matt on top. Matt's right fist lashed out twice, and the soldier lay still. He put on the soldier's hat and jacket and mounted the soldier's horse. The disguise would only work from a distance, but that was all Matt needed at the moment.

As Sam approached his man, the soldier's horse stumbled. He dismounted to check the animal's leg. As he bent over, the horse's hoof in his hand, Sam stealthily edged close, tapped him on the shoulder. Startled, the soldier whirled around right into Sam's closed fist. The soldier's eyes glazed over and he fell, facefirst, into the dirt. Sam also put on the Mexican's hat and jacket and took over his horse.

Both incidents had just taken seconds, leaving two more guards to eliminate. Sam wasted no time, but spurred his borrowed horse toward the third rider. That soldier was smoking a cigarette when he heard the hoofbeats behind him. He turned, expecting to see his fellow soldier. When he saw the American riding toward him, he tried to pull his gun, but he was too slow. Matt rammed his horse into the third rider, jumping out of the saddle at the last second, landing on his feet. The impact knocked both horses to the ground. In seconds, Sam had covered the ground with his long legs and knocked the rider unconscious with a left hook.

Sam glanced toward the prison wagon, saw Matt moving toward the seated guard and driver. He grabbed the reins to the soldier's horse, remounted, and also hurried toward the wagon.

Matt's borrowed horse wasn't as well-trained as his own and made more noise as it approached. The big guard turned to see Matt racing toward him, raised his shotgun, and fired just as Matt paced the wagon and pushed the gun to one side. The buckshot grazed the rear of one of the horses, startling it. The team started running.

The guard tried to aim the gun a second time, but his aim was again off and the shot went harmlessly into the air. Matt and Sam each slid off their horses into the driver's seat at the same time. Matt grappled with the guard, pitting strength against strength for control of the gun. The faces of the two men were just inches from each other. The force being exerted by the two men threatened to bend the gun barrel.

Though the guard was larger, Matt was the more powerful of the two. Matt finally forced the other man slowly to his knees. Jerking the gun from his hands, Matt brought the heavy barrel down on the guard's head, sending him sprawling to the floor.

Sam placed his arm around the driver's neck, cutting off his wind. The driver clutched at his throat with one hand, while trying to hold onto the reins with his other hand. Matt plucked the reins from the driver and expertly slowed and then stopped the prison wagon.

A voice came from inside the wagon. "Hey, what's going on? Is that you, Whaley? You rescuing us?"

Matt leaned over the seat so that his head could be seen, almost upside down, through the side window.

"Good news and bad news, guys! Good news for you is that we're rescuing you from Delgado's men. Bad news is that we're bringing you back across the river to face justice in the States."

Jessup groaned.

"It would have to be you, Sam Two-Wolves!"

"And don't forget Matt Bodine!" Sam added. "He did help a little."

"A little?" Matt said. "We'll see if you feel the same next time you need me to pull your neck off the chopping block!"

"You twisted my arm. Gentlemen, give Matt just as much credit for your rescue as to me!"

"Go to hell," Jessup said.

"Is that gratitude for you, or what?" Sam asked.

"Maybe you could stop gabbing and get up here to help me tie these two!" Matt said. "Then we can get this rig going in the right direction—north, for the border!"

Twenty

Matt held the reins to the prison wagon as it moved slowly across the rough landscape. Sam held a shotgun on the seat beside him, scanning the horizon for the enemy. Tied up at their feet were the two Mexicans who had been driving the wagon. Guns and ammunition captured from the Whaley gang members and the Mexicans were in a box behind the seat.

"I don't like this," Sam admitted. "We're making damned slow progress."

"The border is still a long ways off," Matt agreed. "We could get a little more speed out of these horses, but as heavy as this wagon is, I think they'd tire before we got to the Rio Grande. I'm hoping our luck holds out a little longer and we don't have any company."

The sun was starting to set. It gave the western sky a reddish tint and cast streaked shadows across the ground. A wagon wheel bounced over a rock, temporarily tilting the unwieldy wagon, making it feel as if it would tip over. Matt, who had worked as a shotgun rider at one time, expertly handled the vehicle and didn't give the bump another thought. Grumbling, however, came from inside the wagon.

"We could always lighten the load a little," Matt said.

"Hmmm . . . Which would you prefer? We could lose the members of Whaley's gang that are back there, but then how could we show our faces in Texas again? Josiah would kick us out of the Rangers for not bringing back our men!"

"We gave up being Rangers when we crossed the border," Matt reminded him.

"Details . . . merely details. Josiah would still be mad as a hornet, and I'd rather avoid that."

"Good point. We could also abandon the gold by the side of the road."

"Then we'd have the entire United States government on our backs!" Sam pointed out.

"They could be anyway . . . I suspect we've violated a dozen international laws already. Last we saw Holz and Easton, they were pretty upset."

"Better them than Josiah."

"So what's your suggestion?"

"We could let the Mexican prisoners go." Sam nudged one of the tied-up men, who gave him a dirty look.

"Maybe . . . but I still think they're better off where we can keep an eye on them. We'll let them go before we cross the river."

"Or maybe we could keep them and try for a new record in violating international laws? Wonder what illegality that would be classified as?"

"Wonder what the record is?" Matt mused. "We might have a chance, after all . . ."

Sam hit him with his hat. He grinned, though his other hand never left the shotgun.

The two had been in tight spots before, but never one quite like this. They were in a foreign country, with a wagon full of gold and prisoners taken from the Mexican government, while they were also being chased by the federales . . . with no place to run and no friends to count on. Matt and Sam used the good-natured bantering to try and ease the tension.

The main problem was not the wagon itself but the direction it was headed. It had been headed for Delgado when the blood brothers took it over. Now it was headed north, for the United States. Delgado would eventually question why it did not arrive as expected and send out a party to investigate. Or some of his soldiers might just happen to see the wagon where it was not supposed to be and start to ask questions.

The best hope might be the night. The darkness could help to hide them, though it would do little to silence the squealing wheels turning on the poorly greased axles. On the other hand, this area did not have many people living in it, and the border was only a few miles away.

"How are we doing?" Sam asked.

"Horses are tired. Should make it. Maybe we'll get lucky."

Sam raised the shotgun and pointed it toward the southwest. "No such luck this time. We have some visitors. Looks like maybe a dozen riders coming this way."

Dingo Whaley was so mad he could chew nails. He had already punched holes in the cabin walls with his bare fists and torn the door off its hinges.

"Damned those lying, good-for-nothing, cheating, stealing, good-for-nothing bean-eating bastards." His breath was ragged. "And damned that Delgado for turning on us like that. And especially for taking the gold. I never should have let Jessup talk me into this scheme. It never pays to have partners that you can't control."

"What's the plan, boss?" Pierce said. He nervously fingered his mask that he held in his hands. "I hate to lose these men—even Jessup. They're all a cut above Murdock. He got what he deserved! But these men are all loyal to you."

"Who cares?" He spit. "I want the gold. I want to kill Delgado—tear off his legs and feed them to the dogs and watch him scream. And I want to kill anybody who gets in my way."

Pierce was not about to disagree with Whaley on even a minor point.

"So we go after the gold?"

"How many men do we have left?"

"I figure seven. Not enough to take on an army."

"But enough to take on a prison wagon."

"Yeah. They put the gold in there. And to think we helped them move it!" Whaley glared at Pierce, who quickly changed the subject. "Seven men should do it. If there aren't too many guarding it."

"Have the men saddle up. We're going after our gold."

Delgado sat on his horse and watched the prison wagon making its slow progress—in the

252

wrong direction. He knew that something had gone wrong. He had a gut feeling that something was two men named Matthew Bodine and Sam Two-Wolves. They had eluded him and his men since they had crossed the river and he had unsuccessfully tried to arrest them. This made him very angry.

If Matt and Sam had taken control of the prison wagon, that would mean they were very dangerous, indeed, since they would have had to overcome all the guards. Delgado was tempted to just let those two have the prisoners and go home, just to get rid of them. Unfortunately, the gold was also in the wagon, and that made him even angrier. He could not let that pass.

Delgado decided to send in some of his men to investigate, but he decided to approach cautiously. He would remain a safe distance away, to join his men if needed.

He said, "Sergeant, take a party of men and find out what's going on with that wagon. Do not let it continue toward the river under any circumstances. Bring it back to me."

"Yes, sir."

"Be careful. Those two Americans, Bodine and Two-Wolves, may be involved. If so, they will be dangerous."

"Do you want me to bring them to you, as

well?" The sergeant spoke with puffed-up pride, as if that would be a simple matter.

"I doubt if you'd have the chance to take them alive. If you see them, kill them on the spot—if you can. I'll give a bonus to each man whose bullet marks their bodies." He thought for a minute, then added, "Kill the prisoners, too, if you want, though there will be no bonus for them. These Americans have all become more trouble than they're worth. All I'm interested in now is the gold."

"Who do you figure?" Matt asked, keeping a firm grip on the reins.

"From that direction, I figure it's Delgado's men."

"Looks like we'll have to fight our way out of this one."

"Not necessarily. Maybe we can outsmart them. They're still too far away to see us clearly. Stop the wagon."

Sam climbed down and banged on the bars on the side of the wagon, getting the attention of the three prisoners inside. Jessup looked out at him.

"Think you could make this ride a little rougher?"

"You ought to be glad you're heading for an American prison instead of a Mexican prison. You need to keep that in mind, because we're having some visitors. Delgado's men—maybe some of the same ones that turned on you and imprisoned you."

"I'd like to get a shot at them!" Jessup said.

"We're going to try something, but you boys need to keep quiet. If you don't, you'll be back in the hands of Delgado."

"Give us guns. You may need our help."

"We'll handle it. You just keep quiet."

Sam climbed back beside Matt, reached down, and pulled the gag from the mouths of the two tied-up men. He held his revolver with his other hand just inches from the Mexican's face. Sam spoke in Spanish.

"Here's the deal. You two take your positions. Matt and I will be down here, with our guns aimed straight at your balls. You tell a good story, and you'll keep your family jewels. Screw up, even a little, and your women will be looking elsewhere for their pleasure. You savvy?"

The driver, a wide-bodied man with a thin mustache, nodded energetically. The guard, a tall and muscular man, said simply, "Yes."

Sam untied them. He removed the shells from the shotgun and handed it to the guard. They took their places while Sam and Matt crouched on the floorboard. It was a tight squeeze, but it wouldn't be as tight as a Mexican prison cell or a plot six feet in the ground.

"Continue driving," Sam said. "Move it."

The wagon started creaking again.

"This is your plan?" Matt asked.

"You got a better one?"

"Not at the moment."

"Then don't complain!"

The wagon seemed to move even slower. It took minutes for Delgado's men to reach the wagon, though it seemed like hours to Matt and Sam.

"Hey, Carlos!" one of Delgado's men shouted. "What's going on here?"

Sam pushed the barrel of his gun against the driver's leg. He said, "On our way with the prisoners, Sergeant! I am very, very happy to be going home!"

"But, Carlos, you seem to be going in the wrong direction."

"No . . . no . . . I am going . . ." He looked confused. "Aren't we going back to the *comandante's* headquarters, Hector?"

The guard leaned over slightly and said in a conspiratorial voice, "Carlos has been celebrating a little early! He is a little confused."

"Understandable," the sergeant said. "But inexcusable. Not with what you have at stake here."

Both men shrugged in response.

The rider, suspicious, kicked his horse around the side of the wagon. It was getting dark enough that Matt and Sam figured they probably would not be seen unless he looked specifically for them. So far, he didn't seem to suspect that they were there. He was, however, acting as if he sensed something wrong. He looked the wagon over from a safe distance, then rode in closer, leaning down to get a closer look through the bars. Jessup and the other two prisoners stared at him blankly but said nothing.

"Where are the other guards?" the sergeant finally asked, more forcefully.

The guard cleared his throat as Sam shifted again, nudging him with his gun.

Matt and Sam looked at each other. Neither said a word, but the two had fought together for so long that both knew what the other was thinking. Using subtle hand gestures, the two agreed on their plan of action without having to use a single word.

"Would you care for a drink?" the driver finally asked, beads of sweat on his forehead.

"Step down," the sergeant said, directing his horse to the front of the wagon to join the other men. "Both of you. I don't know what's going on, but I intend to find out—"

Almost as one, Sam and Matt exploded from their hiding places. Sam picked up the driver and Matt picked up the guard from the seats and hurled them from the wagon. The surprised sergeant had no time to react as he saw the two bodies come rushing at him. The driver hit first, knocking him from his horse. The guard flew over both of them, hitting the sergeant's horse. The impact startled him. The horse raised on its hind legs, spooking the other horses. The scene was chaos as men found themselves on the ground, tangled in their gear, while the horses tried to run away.

Sam took advantage of the confusion. He grabbed the reins and hollered at the team. Though the words were English, the four horses seemed to understand and took off immediately in a cloud of dust.

Matt fired a series of shots, sending the rest of the soldiers diving to the ground, looking for cover.

The wagon pitched and rolled over the rough terrain, though Sam kept control.

"What's the plan, now?" Matt yelled over the rushing wind.

"Drive like hell and hope we make it!"

Twenty-one

Sam was also an accomplished driver and kept the heavy prison wagon on course. He coaxed an amazing amount of speed from the four-horse team. From their position on top of the wagon, the passing country seemed to be a blur and it was almost impossible for Matt and Sam to keep their seats. They still managed to hold on as if they were glued to the wagon.

Delgado's men continued to take potshots at them, but they were too far away for the bullets to even get close. A mile passed, then another mile. Finally, the Mexican soldiers started to fall back and Sam slowed the wagon a little.

"Think we lost them?" Matt asked.

"In this rig? Not a chance."

"Yeah. I agree. So what's the deal? Why aren't they still coming at us?"

"Maybe they took a lunch break?"

"Wishful thinking. I could use a break. It feels like I haven't slept for days."

"That sounds about right. Between that and being thumped in the head, I feel like death warmed over. But I've been in worse shape."

"Yeah. We both have. It won't be long now before we reach the river. We can get some rest after this is all over."

"A lot can still happen. I think Delgado is up to something. Let's keep our eyes open."

Josiah Finch woke up in a strange bed, surrounded with smells of antiseptic surrounding him. He raised up, felt the pain in his shoulder, and gave thanks that it hadn't been his gun hand. A Ranger that couldn't shoot would be virtually worthless, and he wasn't ready to retire. He used his free hand to feel his shoulder, noted the smooth bandages.

"Well, Josiah, you messed up this time," he said to himself. "Letting yourself get bamboozled that way . . . not much of an example I sit for myself. Didn't even take out the attacker before I let myself get knocked out. Damn."

"Some say talking to yourself is not a good sign," the voice in the corner said. "Of course, that way you're always guaranteed a good conversation."

"Just my luck . . . I wake up to some smart-ass."

Dr. Stanford smiled. "Smart-ass is my bedside manner. But only for a select few patients."

"And I'm the lucky one?"

"Considering what I had to dig out of you, and considering the blow you received, I'd say you are one hell of a lucky man. I figured you'd be out for a lot longer. And certainly not acting so perky as this. I promised your two friends to stick around until you regained consciousness. Guess now I can go out for a cup of coffee."

"Matt and Sam? They brought me here? I'll have to talk with those boys about being Texas Rangers. They should've been after those yahoos that rode into town."

"Maybe they're Rangers, but first of all they are men. Good men who value their friends."

"Hell, I know that," Josiah said. "I can always count on them to do what they believe to be right, no matter what anybody says and no matter what the consequences. And I know that the gang won't get away from them, like lots of others I know." Finch raised up in bed. "Where in blazes are my clothes?"

"I had to cut your shirt off, since the wood

in your shoulder pushed some of the material into the wound. It was soaked in blood."

"Then find me another, pronto!" Josiah said. "I'm going to help those boys. If I know them, they're already in Mexico in who knows what kind of mess."

"In my professional opinion, you should stay in bed for at least another three days . . ."

"Thanks for your concern, Doc, but I've crossed a hundred mile of desert with a bullet in my lung and climbed half a mountain with infection in my leg. A little splinter isn't going to slow me down."

"I'll get you some clothes."

Delgado watched the prison wagon race toward the horizon. This was becoming an annoying routine, watching that damned prison wagon going where it wasn't supposed to go. When he finally caught up with Bodine and Two-Wolves, he would personally supervise their execution. They had caused him more problems than the entire U.S. army and Texas Rangers had and he was tired of it.

"Sergeant, take a group of men and circle around. I want that wagon cut off from the front, while we come up the rear. You let them get away once. Do not let them get to the river. If you fail this time, you will be the one to suffer."

"Yes, sir."

"We'll put them in a stranglehold from which they cannot escape. Take your best men. Do whatever it takes to stop them. I want the gold. And I want those two Americans dead."

Matt was the first to notice the group of riders in the distance in front of them.

"There's the answer to the mystery," he said. "Delgado had his men circle around, blocking us from the river."

"They're still out of firing range," Sam noted. "We've got a few minutes. Options?"

"Can't turn back. Our only hope is to get to the river. The team is too tired to try to circle around them, even if we had the time. They'd still be able to catch up to us in no time. Looks like we'll have to try and plow through."

"Afraid you'd say that. I know how you admire a well-thought-out, sophisticated, and subtle plan."

"Are you complaining?"

"Hell, no. I came up with the same plan. Great minds think alike."

"These horses have any go left in them?"

"I've been trying to save them as much as possible these past few miles," Sam said. "I'm afraid they're about played out. I might get a little more out of them. It won't be much."

Matt leaned back in the lurching seat, reloaded his revolver and his rifle.

"They're just sitting there, waiting for us," Sam said. "They haven't moved a bit. They're like vultures waiting for us to die."

"There's others behind us, moving in on us. They're trying to surround us."

"When they get in range, I'm going to get these critters to move as fast as they can. You do your best to hang on and shoot straight. Maybe you can cause them some problems."

Somebody from the group behind them fired a rifle. It was a lucky shot, hitting the back of the wagon, though they were so far away that the bullet had no force left.

"Good thing they don't have none of the buffalo rifles like Whaley's gang is so fond of," Matt said. "If they did, we could be in trouble . . ." He paused. "That's it! That could be the answer to our problem!"

Matt climbed behind the seat, lifted the top of the compartment holding the captured weapons of the Whaley gang, including a well-maintained buffalo gun and a supply of shells.

Matt whooped and said, "Brother, we're in business!"

Josiah Finch had exaggerated his stories somewhat, but it had gotten him out of the doctor's office. Riding over the rough terrain did hurt his shoulder and back, but he gritted his teeth and ignored the pain.

When he arrived at the river, Leeds had his men ready for action, though he remained on the American side of the border.

Leeds smiled broadly. "Josiah! Matt and Sam said you were hurt! What are you doing out here?"

"Just a scratch," Finch said. "I'm not going to let a little thing like that keep me out of the fight. I feel kind of responsible for this. If it hadn't been for my plan, none of this might have happened . . ."

"It was a gamble," Leeds said. "Sometimes you win. Sometimes you lose. If you hadn't flushed the outlaws out, they would have eventually done even more damage. As far as I'm concerned, you've done a fine job."

"What's going on now?"

"Matt and Sam crossed the border. I have faith in those two. I'm positive they're going to return with the gold, the prisoners, or both.

So I'm sticking around, in case they need my help."

"I'm going over," Finch said. "Those boys can take care of themselves, but an extra gun never hurts."

"Holz and Easton won't like it."

"Do I look like I'm asking permission? If they don't like it, they can try to have my badge when I get back."

Finch raced his horse to the river and then to the south. He didn't have to go very far before he saw the Mexican soldiers stretched out in a line, their backs to him. In the distance, a prison wagon was hurrying toward them in a large cloud of dust.

"If that's not Matt and Sam, I'll eat my hat!" Josiah chuckled. "I'd like to hear *this* story! Well, I'll just make it a little easier for them."

He pulled his gun, yelled a loud Indian cry that Sam had once taught him, and pushed toward the soldiers. The first one turned and was knocked out of his saddle by a well-timed punch as the Ranger passed. A second soldier shot, but Finch's gun was more accurate. The slug caught the soldier in the neck. He held on the saddle for a few seconds before sliding off to the ground.

In the distance, a large gun boomed and a third soldier clutched his stomach as blood flowed in an uneven pattern, soaking the dirty uniform.

The gun boomed again, and another soldier fell.

Josiah fired his gun twice more at the soldiers that had suddenly broken rank and were almost in a panic.

The prison wagon was moving quickly toward the soldiers. Matt had the buffalo gun loaded and sighted.

"They're still almost out of range," Sam said. "And if you can hit anything from this bouncing outfit, I'll buy you a round at Rosie's."

"Make it two rounds."

"It's a deal." He sighted the gun, when he noted another figure approaching from behind the soldiers. "I'll be damned. Do you see what I see?"

"It could only be one man. But didn't we leave Josiah unconscious in the doctor's office?"

Josiah knocked one rider off his horse and fired a shot, taking out another soldier.

"It's a good start," Matt said. "Let's see how many we can add to the score."

The big gun boomed. Seconds later, another soldier fell.

"I'll be damned," Sam said.

The gun boomed again two more times. Between the buffalo gun and the Ranger, the Mexican soldiers were in chaos. Matt pulled his regular rifle, and peppered the group with bullets as the wagon approached.

The soldiers still on horseback moved to one side and let the prison wagon pass.

Sam slowed the wagon and Josiah came up beside them.

"Thought I might find you boys down here," the Ranger said. "Looks like you've done all right for yourselves."

"We've got the gold as well as some of the Whaley gang," Matt said. "We haven't gotten Whaley yet. But his time will come."

"What about you?" Sam asked. "Here you are, out doing around, and we were actually worried about you!"

"I appreciate the thought, boys. And I appreciate your help. In the meantime, you'll have some help waiting for you at the river. Leeds has his men ready to back you up, as soon as you get on the American side."

"That's good news. Maybe if Delgado leaves us alone for a while, we can actually make it home."

The river was now very close. The smell of water was in the air.

"Almost there," Matt said. "Another few minutes is all we need. And . . . damn."

From the south Matt spotted another cloud of dust. "No sooner do we get rid of Delgado's men than we have more visitors. Looks like this time it's Dingo Whaley himself."

"Here we go again," Sam said. "Hold on. We're heading for the border!"

Twenty-two

The river was within sight. Though the team was tired, Sam continued to bring out the best in them as they rushed toward the water.

Whaley's gang was more bold than Delgado's men had been and were riding so close that Matt could almost touch them. They were wearing masks. The buffalo guns were not practical at such short range. Instead, Matt crouched on top of the wagon, firing both guns at the attackers. Their bullets whistled past him, buried themselves in the wood of the wagon.

Matt glanced toward the front of the wagon, noticed a long line of soldiers across the river: Colonel Leeds and his soldiers were waiting for them, just as Finch had said.

The heavy wagon lurched as the wheels hit

the river. It could have stuck in the mud in the bottom of the river, and would have if not for Sam's talented driving. He had enough momentum going that even though the vehicle paused dangerously for a second, the animals did not stop but kept on as fast as they could go, providing enough force to keep the wagon moving.

The American soldiers moved to one side to allow the wagon to move onto U.S. soil. As the wheels bit into the soft riverbank the feet of one of the horses slipped. The pause was enough that one of the wheels started to sink.

Behind the wagon, Whaley's men continued to shoot. The soldiers fired back, sending the outlaws scurrying for cover in the scrub grass and mesquite.

Sam kept a firm grip on the reins and yelled at the horses, trying to push them past the point of endurance. They gave it their best effort, and the wagon started to give again. The wagon moved, then suddenly lurched free with such force that it tilted.

As if in slow motion, the wagon started to turn over. Matt and Sam leaped for safety. As Sam hit the ground, he fired a single shot at the lock, blowing the metal apart. The door flew open and the prisoners also leaped to safety.

The wagon tottered and fell the remaining several feet. It hit with a loud crash. Pieces of wood and metal for a dozen feet in all directions, sending up clouds of dust. The open door bent at an awkward angle onto itself.

The three prisoners tried to run away, but were stopped at gunpoint by American soldiers.

The wagon was on American soil.

Holz and Easton watched the action on the Mexican side of the river along with Leeds. Like Leeds, they could do nothing to help the blood brothers on the other side.

"They're actually going to make it," Easton said. "Thank God."

"Unbelievable," Holz said.

When the wagon crashed, the two diplomats were among the first to arrive at the scene.

"Matt! Sam! Are you all right?"

"We're fine. Just got some unfinished business to take care of."

"You surely don't mean . . ."

Finch rode up, leading two horses.

"Here they are, boys. Let's get going!"

Holz stepped between the men and the river. "After all you've gone through, do you mean to say you're actually going to cross it—"

A shot echoed from across the river and Holz crumpled. Sam caught the body as it fell. On the other side of the water, Whaley's gun was still smoking. He saw he had hit the wrong person, and ran in the opposite direction.

Holz choked. His face grew slack. A tiny drop of blood oozed from the corner of his mouth.

Sam placed him softly on the ground and said, "You bet we're crossing that river."

In the confusion, Tom had lost sight of the others. He was almost out of ammunition and he was tired. Everything was lost. There was no gold. The Whaley gang was gone, and with it the chance of any future riches. If he returned to the States, he would face jail or worse. His chances in Mexico were not much better.

And to make matters worse, he had lost his horse in the fight. He was walking aimlessly in the hot sun, when he looked up to see the Ranger, Josiah Finch, coming at him.

From the other direction came another rider. Ben was closer and arrived first. He reached down and picked up the other outlaw.

"Stop!" Finch cried out. "You are both under arrest!"

Ben rolled out of the saddle, taking with him the saddlebags with the last of the dynamite. Tom followed Ben's lead. Both tried to hide in small hollows in the ground. Finch also dismounted and hit the ground.

"I'm not going back," Tom said. "You'll have to kill me first. I've seen the last of the inside of a jail cell."

"Don't make it worse on yourselves," Finch said. "You all weren't part of the original Whaley gang. You didn't take part in the worst of the crimes. You all won't be hanged. There's no reason for you to die now."

Tom answered with two shots from his revolver. From another direction, Sam returned the fire. The two men had the outlaws pinned down. There was no way they could escape.

"This is it," Tom said. "The end of the line."

"Not necessarily. I still have this." He held up the final sticks of dynamite. "It's still enough to blow them sky-high."

"I'll have to apologize for all the bad things I thought about you," Tom said.

Ben acted as if he hadn't heard the other outlaw. He lit the fuse and tossed the explosives toward Finch.

"Damn, I hate dynamite!" the Ranger said. He stood, fearlessly, and shot at the explosive package sailing toward him. The bullet hit it, forcing it to another direction. Sam also shot, hit it as easily as if he were shooting tin cans. The dynamite hit the ground a safe distance away and exploded harmlessly.

The outlaws jumped and shot again at the Rangers and ex-Rangers, using the smoke from the dynamite as cover. It wasn't cover enough as the bullet from Finch's gun hit Ben in the gut, doubling him over with pain, and the bullet from Sam's gun hit Tom in the head, just above the right eye.

Each man fell without firing another shot.

Whaley couldn't believe his eyes. Two-Wolves and Bodine had actually done it. They had brought the prison wagon, with the gold and his men, back across the river and into the custody of the Americans.

And now they were coming back to him.

Whaley decided to let his men that were still alive take care of themselves.

He grabbed his horse, tried to step into the saddle, but was stopped by strong arms throwing him to the ground. He rolled and came up ready to fight.

Matthew Bodine was just feet away, looking him straight in the eye.

"By all rights, Josiah should have the pleasure of taking you in," Matt said. "But I reckon I can do the job. He can enjoy your hanging."

"You're a fool, Bodine. Look at you. You're exhausted. You've got a knot on your head the size of a goose egg. You can't beat me. Just let me go and we'll call it even. Otherwise, I'll have to kill you."

"I'm still more man than you'll ever be," Matt said, mocking the gang leader. "Let's see you try me, if you think you're man enough."

Whaley was big, strong, and fast. He moved in and hit Matt with three punches before he could react. And Whaley was right about Matt being tired. He had gone for too long without sleep and his head was throbbing. He didn't need any more punishment, and the blows from Whaley's massive fist sent shudders through his body.

Matt, however, was young and strong and had years of training behind him. He hit Whaley with a strong punch to the stomach, felt like he was hitting iron. Another punch to the chin had better results. It caused the bigger man to pause for a second. Matt took the opportunity to deliver a series of right and left jabs to the face, opening a cut above Whaley's eye.

Angry and now in pain, Whaley lost control as he charged Matt. This was what Matt was looking for. At the last second, Matt sidestepped the charge, grabbed Whaley's hair, and pulled him off-balance. Matt forced Whaley's face into the ground with a bone-jarring crunch.

Blood now streamed down Whaley's face and blood came from the outlaw's broken nose. Still the outlaw came back for more, delivering a solid kick, almost breaking Matt's kneecap. Matt pivoted and came down with two closed fists on the back of Whaley's neck. The blow might have broken a normal person's neck, but Whaley was stronger than most.

He jumped up, tried to get Matt in a bear hug. Again, Matt sidestepped, delivering a backhanded blow as he slipped away.

Whaley stepped back, breathing hard.

"You're a hard man to beat," Whaley said. "But it's time to stop this nonsense."

His hand dropped to his holster. That was Whaley's final mistake. Matt also reached for his gun in a movement so fast that it was almost a blur. Whaley got off a shot that hit the ground in front of Matt. Matt's shot was more accurate, hitting the outlaw leader in the stomach.

Whaley didn't go down, so Matt fired three more times, placing the shots in a tight pattern in Whaley's midsection. He groaned and tumbled to the ground.

Suddenly, all was quiet. Whaley's gang was all dead or wounded.

Sam and Josiah joined Matt as he stood over Whaley's body. Sam and Matt each grabbed one of the outlaw's arms and dragged him across the river, dumping him on the ground in front of Leeds and Easton, near where Holz's body also rested.

Only one or two of the former Whaley gang was still living. The ones that were wounded walked slowly across the river to surrender to the American soldiers. Matt and Sam went back and dragged the other bodies to the American side.

"I think this just about takes care of it," Sam said. "You have the gold. You have all the members of the Dingo Whaley gang."

"I suppose there is also the matter of charges that could be pressed against us for breaking the laws of two countries," Matt said.

"No, considering the circumstances, I'd say you two are in the clear," Easton said. "I might even be able to wrangle some kind of award for you two and Josiah for bringing these cutthroats to justice."

"Nothing like that for us," Sam said.

"And not for me, either," Josiah said. "Not if it means putting on a suit and attending another one of those dinners!"

The Texas countryside was finally quiet.

Leeds pointed one more time to Mexico and to one lone figure riding up to the water's edge."

So, Colonel Leeds, you win this one," Delgado said.

"We have the prisoners. We have the gold. And we have you dead to rights. We know you had a hand in that gold robbery. We know how you protected Whaley's gang."

"I might point out that you have no proof of my involvement. Was I or any of my men actually part of the robbery? You know the answer to that. And as for protection . . . I had Whaley's gang under arrest and confiscated the gold. Who is to say that I wasn't trying to safeguard the gold for its eventual safe return to your government? No, Colonel, you have nothing on me. In fact, I believe I will file a complaint."

"It won't do you any good this time," Leeds said. "You can bluster all you want."

"Yes, I know. Still, one does what he can."

"There'll be some changes coming," Easton warned. "When I get back to Washington, I'll see to that."

"I'm sure there will," Delgado said. "But we'll cross that river when we come to it." He touched the brim of his hat. "Good day, gentlemen. I'm sure our paths will cross again."

Twenty-three

Matt and Sam stood looking at the Rio Grande, holding the reins of their horses. Mexico was on the other side, though it had the same scrub grass and mesquite as the Texas side of the river. The wreck of the prison wagon was still on U.S. soil, where it had landed. The sun had already started to bleach it white.

"So much trouble, so much bloodshed, so many killed, because of this border," Matt said.

"Not just the border," Sam said. "It's the same old story. Greed. Gold. Power. Doesn't make any difference which side of the river you're on. Men are still men, no matter the nationality."

"We've seen it before. I'm sure we'll see it again."

"But we'll handle it, brother. You can count on it."

The two men turned and led the horses toward the camp, where Josiah Finch was talking with Colonel Leeds. His soldiers were relaxing around the camp. Matt and Sam poured coffee into cups and sat around the fire with their two friends.

"All in all, you boys can be proud," Leeds said. "You got the gold back. You broke the Dingo Whaley gang, killing them or bringing them to justice."

"Fine Ranger material," Finch said. "Matt, Sam, I wish you all would reconsider your decision to quit the Rangers. We need more men like you."

"We appreciate the offer," Matt said. "But we just can't be tied down now. Our wandering days are far from over."

"Lots of the country we still want to see—or see again," Sam added. "We'll be back in Texas. You can be sure of that. And if you ever need help, just get word to us. No matter where we're at, we'll find a way to get to you."

"There's also the matter of us working for somebody else—even the government. It's one thing working with you, Josiah. You don't try to keep us reined in. You let us do the job. There's no guarantee that would continue. We'd just as soon keep our freedom."

"I can understand that," Finch said. "If I were in your position, I might do the same thing. There's no guarantee I'll even stay with the Rangers."

"Hell, Josiah, you were just about born a Ranger and will die a Ranger. We know you're already itching to check out that new gang working further south. I'm surprised you're even still here."

"You never know. I might just decide to get into politics and follow Leeds to Washington. Think I'd fit in up there?"

Matt and Sam laughed at the image of Josiah Finch unleashed on the D.C. establishment.

"You and your boys just about caused an international incident as it was," Leeds said. "I'd say even that worked out. Once Easton finally got a handle on the situation, it turned out well. I was surprised that he has some contacts up there, after all. I'll be starting my new position in a few weeks."

"Better you than Josiah!" Matt laughed.

"It'll work out well in another way as well," Leeds said. "Rosie is thrilled. And, even better, Mary has agreed to join us to help put together those parties we'll be required to give. It'll be a good move for everybody."

"Well, Sam, at least you'll have one friend in Washington!" Matt joked.

"Remember, you really do have a friend in Washington," Leeds said, more seriously. "I know you boys don't play politics like lots of people do, but if I can ever be of any help . . ."

"We'll remember," Sam said. "We've learned never to say never. And don't hesitate to call on us. We'll be glad to help, as long as we can stay out here in the wide open spaces, where we belong."

"Where you headed for now, boys?" Finch asked.

"May head north," Matt said.

"Or further west," Sam said.

"Whichever way the wind blows."

Leeds stood. "Thanks for the coffee, Josiah. My men and I are headed back to Fort Concho. And thanks again, Matt and Sam, for your help."

The wind blew softly across the river as Leeds had his men mount up and then ride away. The dust rising behind them clouded the sun.

Josiah Finch helped Matt and Sam break camp, shook hands one final time. All three mounted and started to ride, when Finch suddenly stopped his horse and called back.

"Matt! Sam!"

He raced back toward the two blood brothers, who also hurried to meet him.

"What is it, Josiah?" Sam asked.

"Something important I need to tell you," Finch replied.

"What is it?"

"Will you boys this time *please* try and stay out of mischief?" He laughed, slapped his hat against his leg, and then rode away, laughing some more.

Matt and Sam watched their friend until he was out of sight, and then until even his dust had vanished.

"Josiah Finch may be small, but he's more of a man than most of us could ever hope to be," Sam said.

"True," Matt agreed. "But one thing I'm not sure I like about him."

"And what's that?"

"He gives advice that's damned difficult to follow! Imagine *you* staying out of trouble! If not for me, I hate to think where you'd wind up . . ."

"Me? That's funny. Hell, I've lost track of the times I've had to pull you out of the frying pan . . ."

"Into the fire?"

"Which reminds me . . . Whose turn is it to cook this time?"

Matt and Sam laughed again and rode past

the remains of the prison wagon toward the
new adventures waiting for them just down
the road.

FOR THE BEST OF THE WEST, SADDLE UP WITH PINNACLE AND JACK CUMMINGS . . .

DEAD MAN'S MEDAL	(664-0, $3.50/$4.50)
THE DESERTER TROOP	(715-9, $3.50/$4.50)
ESCAPE FROM YUMA	(697-7, $3.50/$4.50)
ONCE A LEGEND	(650-0, $3.50/$4.50)
REBELS WEST	(525-3, $3.50/$4.50)
THE ROUGH RIDER	(481-8, $3.50/$4.50)
THE SURROGATE GUN	(607-1, $3.50/$4.50)
TIGER BUTTE	(583-0, $3.50/$4.50)